The Faintly
Beating Heart

A Prequel to The Sacrifice of One

Emily Fortney

Edition: 1/2022

ISBN: 978-0-9966824-3-5

Cover Design by: www.ebooklaunch.com

Editing by: www.ayersedits.com

Find Emily online at www.emilyfortney.com

TO SARAH, MY FIRST FAN

Battlefield

The Faintly
Beating Heart

CHAPTER ONE

HAND TO THE ground, I felt the earth shake with the sound of the approaching army. The thought thrilled me. My fingers grazed the brown earth as the wind whirled and twisted the threads of grass into matted lumps. To my right sat my home village. A clearing outside our village gate stretched in front of me. Where the clearing touched the tree line was a narrow road that, if traveled, led to our capital city, LilyAye.

I reached into my pocket and retrieved a book small enough that it fit in my hand. The cover was a dusty brown and it had aged so that the title was no longer visible. From between its pages, I pulled out a dried flower. Its petals were blue and featherlike. It was so delicate my fingers barely made contact when I touched the flower.

"Son."

Shoving the book back in my pocket, I turned to look at the old man behind me. I bore an uncomfortable resemblance to my father, John Duffy.

His stocky build, square jaw, and wide nose, all mirrored me, but that day John Duffy's face was drawn with worry while mine held a devilish grin.

My heart beat with excitement at the impending battle. Fighting was a way for me to purge the hurt I felt over Belle. It was the balm I needed to soothe my broken spirit. It was just an added benefit that the army galloping toward us deserved the fury I was ready to dole out.

"Son," my father repeated.

I used my sword to push myself to my feet.

"I would like to talk to you before things are under way." Always short on conversation, he rarely spoke a word, let alone a sentence, without thinking through each pause and inflection.

Turning to face my father, I watched the crowd of men milling around a few yards away. They were my father's men, officially called the Duffy Rebellion.

My father placed a hand on my shoulder. "Are you certain you want to do this?" I blinked at him, trying not to seem too annoyed.

"Yes. Of course." I considered if there was another way to make my voice sound more solid, more sure.

"I won't begrudge you if you go home. You could look after your mother."

"And be seen as a coward? No. I'm needed here. This is what matters right now."

My father nodded to show he agreed, but I knew he hoped I would change my mind.

"Knox," he sighed. "It is easy to *say* that you stand for something." He pulled his hand off my shoulder to rub the bottom of his chin. "It may even be easy to preach your beliefs, but it takes ..."

My eyes drifted back to the group of men. Neil stood awkwardly away from the others.

"It takes a courageous man to act out his beliefs, and an even stronger man to stay standing when things get difficult." My father saw my focus drift. "Knox—"

"I know, Father. I know all of that. We're standing up for what's right, defending our territory."

I'd been hearing that sermon my whole life. It always seemed funny to me that no matter my age, my father was still able to speak to me as if I were a twelve-year-old boy. I was actually twenty-four years old when he leaned in to give me that talk. Maybe it was because I hadn't yet married or fathered any children that he felt he needed to give me these speeches.

"I considered this matter for a long time before coming to the decision to challenge our Supreme Ruler. We don't want to lead these men into danger without just cause," my father said.

My body felt jittery. "We're doing what's right."

"That may be true, but it doesn't change the severity of our mission."

I nodded my head to show him I truly understood. It was a rote action, something I was used to doing to put an end to his ramblings.

"I may not return to your mother." He patted my shoulder where his hand had been resting. His words washed over me. All I could think about was the impending fight and Neil, pompous Neil.

"Don't bother Neil," he said when he saw me staring. "It's not his fault you and Belle didn't end up together."

I bit my lower lip. "I know."

"It's been almost a year, son. It's time to let that part of your life go."

I cared about Belle too much to just *let it go*. Of course, I couldn't say that to my father because it would only lead to another lesson, one about love and jealousy. Neil laughed as someone in the group made a joke.

"What's got you so ruffled today?"

"Nothing," I lied.

I continued to stare at Neil as my father turned to walk away. "When do you think they will arrive?" I called back to him. My father gave me a flat smile.

"Soon," he said. "Knox?"

I moved my focus back to my father.

"Don't be so anxious to invite trouble into your life."

I resisted an audible sigh. The force traveling down the capital road was trouble, but we were there to stop it. He was wrong about Neil. It *was* Neil's fault that I didn't have Belle for myself. I did feel a bit irritated that day. One thing was good about my irritation, it allowed me to no longer hold any hope for Belle. I only needed to convince myself of that.

Neil began fidgeting with his fingernails. I almost didn't approach him, but I felt my feet moving before I could make the decision to go back. Neil had thick, reddish hair that seemed to mound up on his head like drifts of snow. He had a long face and big forehead. I liked to imagine that Belle was always on the brink of laughter every time she looked at her husband's visage.

When he saw me approach, Neil put his hand out to shake mine while at the same time keeping his eyes pointed toward the ground.

"Are you ready?" I asked.

My voice was low and drawn as I took his hand firmly in mine. I was certain that Belle had shared with her husband the details of the relationship we once had, but Neil never treated me any differently.

"I'll admit, I'm nervous. I'd like to stop shaking." Neil finally tilted his head up to look me in the face. "Wouldn't want the enemy getting a hearty joke out of my nerves." Laughter bubbled up from his soft belly as he tried to make light of his fear.

My mouth was tight. My brows furrowed. He made it too easy. Neil's body was paunchy, and despite the mounds of hair, I noticed every time I looked at him, his forehead seemed to grow bigger as his hairline ebbed.

"Maybe you should go home then," I said. "No shame in it."

"And leave you without a redhead to distract them?" Neil turned to look back at the men of the Duffy Rebellion. "All I have to do is run around in circles and they'll get tired from staring at this mess!"

"What about Mirabelle?"

"I had thought of asking her to come and stand with us." He laughed again at his own joke.

"What about the baby?" My tone was still serious.

When Neil saw that I didn't smile, his face relaxed. He looked back down at the ground and a huge smile slowly spread across his face.

"So she *is* with child?" I asked, hoping Neil would admit it was a rumor.

"How did you know?"

"Mirabelle told me."

Belle did not tell me. She did tell my sister, though, who told me. I was sure that Belle was too afraid to tell me in person. Or maybe she just didn't think I was important enough to tell.

Some would say this was the information I needed to let Belle go and move on. I knew watching her belly grow over the next several months would be torture.

Neil scratched at an itch on his arm. "I ... I ... just want to say thank you," he said.

"For what?

"I know you and Belle once loved each other. All of Bear Gap knew it!" Neil laughed nervously. "I just want to thank you for still caring for her. I hope someday, when you have a family, our children will play together. You're a good man, Knox."

Neil met my eyes and I felt like my body would turn to water and wash away. Somehow, despite Neil's odd looks and quirky behaviors, I found myself jealous of him. But there was one opinion I held that would never change. Neil was a fool for fighting that day. As much as I craved the feel of a sword in my hand, if Belle had been mine, I would have run home to be with her that moment.

"She's a strong woman, Knox," Neil continued. "Stronger than me. You don't need to worry about her or the baby."

"Yes, she is." Perhaps she was stronger than me too.

My father corralled his group of about two hundred men. We were mostly all village men not skilled with fighting but lovers of our home territory. My father was the quiet type of leader. Other men saw his passion and just gravitated toward him.

Not every family in Bear Gap supported the rebellion. Some were afraid to challenge a Supreme Ruler. Some, like my sister's husband, didn't want to raise arms against someone else. I held no such belief.

The man who shows his weapon first is the one with the power.

John Duffy stepped back a few paces from us and began to speak. "I remember the day, many months ago, when word spread to our territory about the death of our Supreme Ruler, Bradac. When you hear of something like this, you mourn. When I learned how Bradac died, I did not mourn for the man, I mourned for our nation." Fists flew into the air as a few men whooped and shouted. My father stretched out his arm. His voice rose to a fevered pitch. "Traveling down the capital road right now is the man who assassinated Bradac." His finger quivered as he pointed toward the tree line. It was one of the few times I ever saw my father look truly angry. "Quinten Warwick." My father almost spit the words. "And now the Warwicks have come to our territory of Bear Gap to change things. Do you want a Warwick ruling?" No's popped through the crowd, chased by more shouts.

In Elmyra, the wealthiest was named ruler because the wealthiest was usually the person who had gained the most respect, but that wasn't the case with Quinten Warwick. He seemed to fill his moneybags and build his army in one night.

Off in the distance, one of our men pushed his horse down the capital road toward us, breaking through the tree line. At full speed, he skidded to a stop next to my father.

"They're here," he breathed. "There's more than we thought."

CHAPTER TWO

FROM THE FAR end of the clearing, a line of about twenty Warwick soldiers trotted into the field. Their bodies were stiff, stately. Behind them rode another row of soldiers, chased by a third and a fourth. They were clad in black leather vests. I threw my hand up to block the flares that glinted off the divots in their hammer-formed helmets.

As they drew closer and the marching grew louder, I noticed every man was equipped with a long sheathed sword and spear. Quinten Warwick had brought a small army.

"A hundred men," I muttered. "We can take them with ease."

Our new Supreme Ruler had militias stationed in almost all of the other six territories in Elmyra. Plus he had his guards back in the capital. Elmyra was a big nation that Quinten was trying to control. Bear Gap, although large in land, held only one community and had the least amount of people living there. It made sense that he wouldn't bring the full cavalry just for a small village rebellion.

"Let's stay tight," my father yelled.

He searched for me in the crowd. I pushed forward, jostling my comrades so I could stand next to him. The caravan pressed on us like fog rolling off a lake. The day was hot and I felt a sudden flush of excitement trickle from my forehead down to the tips of my fingers, which traced the handle of my sword. Months of talking, reading, and, rallying had built me into a mad frenzy.

The Warwick army grew close enough that I could see a W burned into the busts of their vests. The first row of soldiers came to a stop and my father was forced to crane his neck to meet the eyes of Quinten.

"Quinten Warwick?" my father asked, his voice steady but small.

"Ridley!" Quinten shouted over his shoulder. "I think this is our welcoming party!"

Laughter rumbled across the sea of Quinten's men. He turned back to face us, his smile broad and flashy. I'd have thought him a cheerful man if it weren't for his other features: dark hair, dark scruffy beard, and dark smoky circles under his eyes.

"You'll call me My Supreme Ruler." Quinten's smile faded.

"Is this the representation for your territory?" Quinten asked. "We have ridden very far south to come somewhere that's this sparse."

"We are few, but we are faithful," my father said. He took a poignant step closer to Quinten's horse. "None of the men behind me will refer to you as Supreme Ruler and neither will I." My father turned to look at his men. I shouted in agreement along with the others as we created a chorus of rebellious cheers. "We'll call you Quinten, no title, no salutation." My father turned back to meet Quinten's eyes and then spat on the ground in front of him.

Quinten laughed lightly. "Well, I suppose I needn't ask why you're standing here." His eyes narrowed as he stared at my father. It was as if he studied an ant crawling through the grass. "Why don't you tell me your grievances." Leaning back in his saddle, Quinten let out a sigh.

None of us expected a rational response to our stand. I looked up at Quinten's army. Every soldier was firm and still, their faces covered with thick helmets that only had slits for the eyes. My father hesitated before answering.

"We only wish to keep our territory the way it is. The people of Bear Gap are happy to live simple lives. We hear you plan to use these lands for your agricultural initiative. We don't want our lands filled with your soldiers."

"Why is it that everyone in this nation thinks that change is a terrible thing?" Quinten said, dropping a hand from his horse's reins. "The Beloved Bradacs ruled for centuries and nothing ever changed!"

Quinten pulled on the bottom of his black vest. All of his men wore a decorative vest over their armor, but Quinten hardly wore any armor. His vest was tight against his chest, wrapping around his thin, muscular frame.

"Some people like the life they've always led," my father said.

"So even when there are problems, everyone still wants the problems to continue?" Quinten looked past my father to the rest of our crowd. His eyes rested on me as he waited for someone to answer the question. "Is this the way of peasants? To continue to live in the mire that you've always lived in?"

"You have no claim to the throne!" I shouted when I noticed my father struggling for words. Quinten's eyes locked on me and I felt everyone in the field staring, including my father. "You stole the reign from the Bradacs!"

"Stole? The Bradacs were careless enough to let me take it! I have every right to my throne and this army behind me will all agree." His army looked strong, but were they really as large as we had feared? Even if these were only a portion of the men supporting Quinten in the whole nation, then we weren't that terribly outnumbered. It actually made me feel embarrassed for him.

Quinten turned his head toward the town as if to take a moment to calm himself. "Hunger plagues small villages just like yours. People are dying from a disease that can be easily cured. So yes, when you hear rumors of my agricultural initiative, I do plan to use these lands, my lands, to save many people. I am so wearied from traveling all these forests and mountains to visit with people, just to have them grumble and try and stop me from claiming what is rightfully mine!" Quinten's voice echoed across the open field. "I am your Supreme Ruler! I rule because I have earned it and I will make the decisions."

My father bent down to pick up a stray piece of dried grass and began chewing on it. "A good ruler listens to his people."

"No. A good ruler makes decisions that benefit the majority," Quinten said. "Now step aside."

"We won't let you into our territory." My father's hand shook as he reached up to grab the reins of Quinten's horse.

Leaning in toward my father, Quinten said, "Did you really think I would listen to a dirty, uncivilized lot, like you?" He sat back up in his saddle and addressed the whole crowd. "I have a plan for this territory that surpasses your understanding. If some of my men die, it will be worth it in the end." The Supreme Ruler moved to place his hand on the hilt of his sword. "And if some of your men die, it will be worth even more. Now, step aside."

Quinten's horse bucked as if reacting to its rider's readiness. My father gripped the reins tighter. He reached for his own sword. The heat pressed in on me as the crowd of men pushed and shuffled. I felt like I were a pot of water ready to boil over into the fire.

"Get off of our land!" someone yelled from behind me.

My teeth were tight as I drew my sword and crossed it in front of my chest.

"You are so foolish! You would rather die than submit to your ruler."

"It is the way of peasants," I spat.

Quinten cocked his head, a signal to his army. Every soldier drew their sword from its sheath, one right after another. It looked as if a ripple bubbled through Quinten's men. They had been a pond and he was the dropped pebble that disturbed the water around it. Quinten paused, giving us a moment to reconsider, back down, or challenge the new Supreme Ruler of Elmyra. We chose the latter.

The sound of my deep, battle cry echoed across the field as I swung my sword at Quinten. For a moment he was surprised, but then he smiled as he struck back at me. My sword met his and I felt the true force of a hit as it reverberated down my sword and into my arm. Behind me metal clashed together our two teams plowing into each other.

Quinten raised his arm high to swing down and split my head open from the top. I knelt, throwing my sword up to block his swipe. Quinten was not a graceful or swift fighter but he was wild and strong.

Our men infiltrated from the center, taking down horses and soldiers as they went. My father fought next to me, a powerful fighter for a man in is fifties. A smile formed inwardly as I started to feel relief at having them outnumbered. They all had horses, but we were fighting at least two to one. We tackled the mounted soldiers, pulling them down and commandeering their horses. Our victory felt near, yet Quinten still fought me, completely unperturbed.

A rumble grew in the forests surrounding us, the sound of many feet hitting the soft grass. On all sides of the field, hordes of men emerged from the trees and charged us. From above me, Quinten laughed. Each new soldier wore a black vest. I searched for my father, wanting his direction, but he was lost now in the battle. Quinten's horse whinnied and bucked.

"You tricked us!" I shouted.

Quinten let the jubilee of his deception show on his face.

Feeling the pressure of the newly dispatched army, I decided to run. I would get out of the middle of this and attack from behind. Horse's hooves pounded succinctly behind me. Quinten was chasing me.

I ran toward the tree line where the field grew into a small peak. He was soon too close for me to outrun.

I stopped suddenly, letting Quinten ride ahead of me a few paces. Turning around, he had sheathed his sword and pulled his spear up into the crook of his arm. His smile taunted me. Quinten turned about to face me again and started riding toward me head on. I ducked, missing the spear, but got clipped by the horse's back hoof. My leg twisted and I fell backward, squinting as the sun flashed in my eyes. I threw my hand up to shield the sun and saw a glint off the tip of the spear. At the last moment, I rolled away from the spear but got caught under the horse's feet. My sword flailed, catching anything it could until it felt like a boulder had smashed into my leg. The sword slipped from my hand and I reached down to grasp my knee. When I opened my eyes, the horse stumbled to the ground, a few large gashes carved into its stomach. I rolled onto my side, feeling blood crawl through the spaces between my fingers.

I was immobile, crippled by pain. The worse torture was the scene laid out in front of me: the Battle of Bear Gap. Below in the clearing, just before the entrance into town, I watched my comrades as they were slaughtered. I felt helpless. The fire that surged inside me went out and I wished we had never challenged Quinten Warwick.

My head felt explosive with hot pain and I screamed. Clawing at the grass, I was overwhelmed with my curse to watch men die with no way for me to rescue them. One of our men fought face-to-face with a Warwick soldier until a sword was driven through his middle and his life ended. Another man, who fought with no weapon, took on a Warwick soldier with his bare hands. He moved swiftly, but his life, too, was ended when he was knocked to the ground. We were outnumbered, painfully outnumbered.

Neil's red hair caught my eyes. He ran across the field, a soldier in pursuit. I clenched my eyes shut, unable to watch any longer. When I reopened them, my father was running toward me.

"Father!"

A noise from behind me drew my attention, and when I craned my neck, Quinten emerged, rising from the ground. He picked up his spear and stepped toward me, cocking his arm back. I turned to face my father again, screaming out with shallow breath. My father lunged at Quinten just as the spear left his hand. The spear's aim shifted to the left so that the tip landed right next to me, splitting open my bicep. Blood poured from my arm. I sat up quickly. My father punched Quinten, knocking him backward. Quinten elbowed him in the face, then grabbed at his hair, shaking my father's head violently. I forced myself to my feet.

"I'm coming," I mumbled.

I took two steps toward my father. My head turned cloudy. I looked down at my arm, now coated in sticky blood. The sun prickled the skin on my forehead. My eyes swam and I reached for a steadiness inside myself that I couldn't find. Quinten barraged my father with hit after hit. I took a third step. My knee buckled. Everything in my world turned black before my body hit the ground.

CHAPTER THREE

MY KNEE RADIATED a pain that felt like hot iron pokers stabbed down to the bone. When I opened my eyes, I was staring at the sky, flat on my back. The day had not turned fully dark yet, but the moon was just visible. I sat up, feeling a sudden burst of nausea. Turning on my side, I vomited violently. My knee was wrapped and so was my arm. I couldn't even remember injuring my arm. There were trees surrounding me, like a silent band of guards. It was so quiet I registered the sound of rustling leaves. The temperature had dropped, but my head still blazed with heat. My face felt sweaty and I started to feel sick again.

I shuffled over to the closest tree, using the trunk to lift me to my feet. The hot stabs ran up my knee the whole length of my leg. Covering my mouth with my forearm, I muffled a scream. I hobbled from tree to tree until I saw the clearing ahead. When I stepped into the field, even in the low light of dusk, I could see that it was strewn with bodies. My breath caught in my throat and dizziness began to overtake me.

Leaving the support of the tree, I struggled to keep my balance. The tough strands of grass wrapped around my ankles as I stumbled through the devastated battlefield. I searched. I searched face after bloodied face for my father's features. Even in my weary pain, one thing was clear in my mind; there was nothing living out there anymore.

Then firelight caught my eye. It was coming from the other side of the field. I squinted to make out the form of a camp. The Warwick army laid their heads that night no more than a quarter of a mile from the people they had just killed. My stomach began to churn again. I needed to get home, away from the memory and away from the place where I knew I would lose my mind.

***

I fell into the thick, wooden door of my parents' house. My fingers were so slippery with blood and sweat that I struggled with the handle. When I finally got it open, I exploded into the house, crashing to the floor. I no longer lived at my parents' house, but this was where my mother and Rebekah were hiding out. I had a small twinge of hope that my father was already here when I saw my mother barreling toward me.

"John! Where's John?" she screeched. "Where is your father?" My mother joined me on the floor, taking my face roughly in her hands. She asked me over and over, "What happened to John? Where is your father?"

"Mother, Knox is hurt," my sister said, but my mother was unfazed.

Her eyes stayed fixed on me, even while Rebekah plucked me from the floor and sat me on a chair. I reached out and grabbed Rebekah's arm.

"You haven't seen Father?" I asked.

"No." Rebekah shook her head quickly. "Knox ..." She bent to look at my knee. "Your knee, what happened?" Gingerly, she touched the crude wrapping that was now soaked through with blood. "Never mind, I'll go get something to clean you up." She stumbled over her words and I wondered if I looked worse than I knew.

"We need to leave," I said, my hand still clutching Rebekah's arm. "It's not safe to stay here."

"Leave? Knox, look at yourself!"

"We ... we ... we can't stay." My words slurred as they left my mouth.

"Where is John?"

"Mother, please," Rebekah said. As gently as she could, she unclasped my hand from her wrist. "There is no way we can leave now."

When Rebekah stole away to the kitchen, my mother came to my side, kneeling next to me like a beggar. "When is your father coming home?" she asked, quieter and meeker than she was before.

I put my hand on top of my mother's hand, but her face remained unchanged. I looked at the blue fabric covering the arm of the chair I sat in. It was my father's chair. Rebekah sat me in my father's favorite chair. I felt a sudden sting of guilt.

Rebekah rounded the corner back into the sitting room. I turned my head slowly, and although she had been quiet for a moment, my mother still stared at me expectantly.

"I think he's dead," I said.

My voice was not my own, shallow and cracked. I spoke the words I was afraid to even think. It ripped at my insides and I began to feel a tightness in my chest. My breaths came quick and flat. It felt impossible to bring air to my lungs. Rebekah gaped at me, a bowl of warm water in her hands. I waited for my mother to wrap her warm arms around my neck and hold me close to her. How desperately I wanted her to comfort me, but she never did. Her face looked as dead as the wood-planked floor. When she stood from my side, horror took over her expression. She moved like a spirit, floating away from me until she was intercepted by Rebekah.

"Mother?" Rebekah asked.

"He's dead." The words spilled out of my mother's mouth like bitter vinegar.

"Don't say that. We don't know that." Rebekah placed a hand on my mother's arm, but she didn't seem to register the touch. "C'mon, Mother, let me take you to bed."

Placing the bowl of water on the end table next to me, Rebekah led my mother to the back bedroom. I stared as the water in the bowl swayed. My head felt foggy and the room around me seemed to dim and fall away. Despite my intense desire to stay awake and alert, my eyelids closed.

I woke up briefly just to look down and see that Rebekah was wrapping my knee, and then again when she cleaned out the cut on my arm. Then a noise pulled me once again out of restless sleep. This time when I awoke, I was wrapped in a blanket and it was dark outside.

"What was that?" Rebekah asked, sounding as if she had been pulled from a nightmare. She sat up from her makeshift bed on the floor next to me.

I listened closely to the hollowness of my parent's home. The fire burned at a low crackle and a gust of air hugged tightly against the outside walls.

"Nothing. Just the wind," I said.

I sat forward. Bringing my hand to my forehead, heat and perspiration radiated off my head like steam.

"What's wrong with your head?" Rebekah crawled out from under her blankets. "Are you hurt on your head?"

"No. My face is just hot."

My sister placed the back of her thin hand on my cheek.

"You have a fever. I'll get you some water to drink."

"I'm all right," I said, falling back to rest my head on the chair.

Focused, selfless acts came naturally to Rebekah but this time she didn't move. Maybe it was from exhaustion, or maybe because of the question that hung in her mind.

"Knox." All I saw was the outline of her body in this house full of shadows. "Did you see what happened to father?"

I blinked at the dark room. "No."

"Are you sure he's not been captured?"

"I don't think the Warwicks make a practice of taking prisoners."

Rebekah shifted on the floor.

"What happened out there today?"

"We were so foolish. Quinten tricked us."

"What do you mean?"

"We didn't have a chance and he knew it. He hid all of his men in the woods so we didn't know what we were getting into." I turned my head, coughing into my arm. "I think our spy was trying to warn us, but we just …"

"Just?"

"We fought anyway."

There was a pause as Rebekah considered my words.

"Do you think we're safe here? In town, I mean."

"I don't know if we're safe," I said honestly. "We could flee to my house. It's out of town, somewhat hidden. It's probably best to stay inside for now."

Rebekah's eyes flickered to the window as if she might have seen a Warwick soldier march past that moment.

"I shouldn't have told Marc to stay at home," she said, pulling her knees up to her chest. "He has no idea what's going on and I'm afraid he'll try and sneak over here tonight with Johnny."

Rebekah was not without her own set of worries. She was married with a little boy of her own. When she decided to stay with our mother during the battle I don't think she imagined it could be as bad as it was. I don't think she knew how hard it would be to be separated from her husband.

"You should have stayed with him."

Her head snapped around as if she were offended but she continued to speak in her normal, flat, matter-of-fact tone.

"You ought to be grateful I was here. I needed to stay and wait with mother, but I couldn't risk having Johnny here in case something went wrong. I don't want him to see all of this."

That I did agree with.

"You look ill," she said, crawling closer to me. "You need to drink."

Rebekah pushed herself off the floor and headed for the kitchen. The whole scene made me feel like a child, my sister and I, fully grown, yet sleeping in the same room at our mother and father's house. Rebekah returned and handed me a mixture of water and herbs to drink. I didn't question the concoction and drank it down in four gulps.

"Check on mother," I called as she took the empty cup back to the kitchen. It was not exactly a request, but Rebekah and I had the type of relationship that didn't need pleasantries.

I heard the clank of one of my mother's clay cups as Rebekah filled it with water from the pitcher in the kitchen. Sleep overtook me momentarily and I didn't even remember her placing the cup on the table next to me. Then I woke to Rebekah's strong hands shaking me awake.

"Mother is gone. Mother is gone!" she said so clearly I understood her in my sleepy delirium.

CHAPTER FOUR

REBEKAH PACED THE floor of my parents' house.

"She kept saying, 'Where is he? Where's John? Where's your father?' It was the same things she had been muttering before I laid her down," Rebekah said.

"Find me a weapon."

"You can barely walk!"

"Find me ..." I gripped the wall for balance, "...a weapon."

"Where could she have gone?"

She could have gotten scared and walked off. Maybe she was wandering the woods of Bear Gap looking for my father. She could have been captured or kidnapped, although I couldn't think of a reason why. These scenarios cycled through my head while I bent to tie another rag around my knee, but I couldn't say any of them to Rebekah. Not because she was too frail to handle it, just because I had no solution to follow up with the problem.

"I don't know," I said, taking a few staggered steps to the door. My knee felt stiff. I could barely walk.

"You're not going out there alone." Rebekah's arm flew in front of me, blocking the door. Her face was a mix of determination and crippling worry.

I swayed back a few inches. My lips fell into a hard line. "Get me a weapon," I repeated, my eyes widening to show I was serious.

Rebekah's eyes were watery. She paused for a moment as if she were going to argue and then turned on her heels to the back of the house.

"Father left this," she said a few moments later. Rebekah held a small dagger in her hand. "I should be the one looking for her."

"No."

"You're hurt and feverish; you can't, Knox."

I was about to rip the dagger from her hand when I changed my mind. If I met any danger, I wouldn't be able to survive hand-to-hand combat with the condition I was in. There was another weapon my father owned that I wanted.

"Keep that on you at all times," I said. "Father wanted you to be able to protect yourself, so you should keep it."

Rebekah pulled the dagger close to her, holding it against her belly.

"Knox, I think-"

"What?"

"What if she went to find Father?"

I took a deep breath and it felt like every part of my body shifted. "Stay here in case she comes back. Keep that dagger close to you."

***

In my father's shed, I found the bow he made when he was a boy. It wasn't hard to find. My father was always an organized man. I pulled the bow and the quiver off a hook on the wall. The wood was splitting and no longer smooth, but the string, which father replaced every year, was still in good shape.

Running my hand over the curved bow, I thought about the first time my father let me hold it. As every young boy does, I begged him to let me come along when he went hunting. When I was six years old, he had taken me out with him one evening. He showed me how to place the arrow and then pull back and aim.

My throat tightened. Suddenly, every memory I had of my father became present in my mind. I brought my fist to my mouth. I was falling apart, ready to give up.

Looking at the bow and quiver in my hand, I swallowed my grief, then swung them over my shoulder and headed into town. The moonlight created a deep gray hue across the village. Walking down the main road, I didn't cross paths with another person. The townspeople were buried away in their homes, terrified to look out their doors or peer through a window.

The more I thought about Rebekah's words, the more I knew she was right. My mother needed closure. She needed to see her husband and know he was dead. I kept picturing my mother traversing the battlefield, blood soaking her feet, the smell ... And it made me walk faster.

I approached the mouth of our territory, a small wooden gate that was usually pulled shut at sunset. That night, the gate hung open. Each step into the field made my knee scream. I ignored the pain. The moon beamed down, alighting all of the bodies and scars left in the battlefield. I walked cautiously, sidestepping my dead friends and neighbors and Warwick men. This was harder than I thought. It was like I had committed a crime, a horrible crime that I regretted, and I was forced to return to the scene and stare at all the filthy, disturbing things I had done.

The field was flat except for a small incline in the middle that seemed higher than it was earlier that day. I collapsed at the top, my knee unable go any further. This was as far as I knew to come anyway. To my left was the patch of woods where I woke up, so my father's body couldn't be too far from there. On the other side of the incline, way over by the capital road, was the Warwick camp. Everything seemed quiet except for a few dying fires. I surveyed the field behind me; the edges of the woods were dark even with the bright moon.

A scream split through the sound of my own heavy breathing. I reached for the bow, my head darting, searching for the source. Pushing my body all the way up to the crest, I looked down to the other side of the field, the side of the Warwick camp, and saw my mother. She was just a silhouette but I could tell she was on her knees.

A Warwick soldier grabbed her by the wrist and pulled her to her feet. My whole body clenched. I whipped an arrow out of the quiver, setting it in the bow. The soldier shook my mother like a limp child's doll. Focusing my vision, I straightened the arrow and pulled back. Sweat rolled over my eyebrow and into my eye. The soldier tossed my mother back onto the ground and I released the arrow.

The arrow found its mark on the soldier's shoulder. He cried, falling backward. A few paces back from the soldier, a horse rode up with a woman atop it. I wouldn't have known it was a woman except that a head of long, curly hair flowed around the edge of her cape. The hood around her head cast dark shadows on her face. I started to second guess myself. Was that man a Warwick soldier? I squinted my eyes to look harder. The woman jumped off her horse, but before she could tend to the soldier, her head snapped around and her eyes focused on me. I felt a jolt of uneasiness. The woman was unarmed, so I grunted to my feet and ran down the hill toward my mother.

"Mother!" I yelled. Her head popped up.

The battlefield fell away as I focused on my mother. Suddenly, all I could hear was my father's voice in my head. This thing, this battle was serious. My feet stopped a pace from my mother and I looked into her eyes, wet and rimmed red.

"Knox," she muttered.

Then I felt the strangest of pains. It was so odd and consuming I forgot about my knee. It started as a pinprick in the center of my chest, light but irritating. I reached up with my left hand to push away whatever was plaguing me, but there was nothing.

"Knox?"

The pain grew like ripples in a stream. Burning filled my entire body with the epicenter being my heart. I clutched at my chest, feeling my heart beat fast and loud, like the banging of a hammer. I screamed out, dropping the bow and quiver.

"What?" I mumbled. "St-stop."

I looked at mother until she turned to her right, where the caped woman was standing. My eyes followed hers as the woman pressed toward me slowly, her hand raised with a flat palm. The pain deepened with every step she took until it over came me and I fell backward.

"Knox!"

The stars sparkled at me and the bright moon was my companion. This was where I thought I would die. Every element of my body felt as if it were ending, giving up.

A strand of dark, wavy hair intruded my view of the sky. The woman's features were soft, her hair feminine and beautiful. Her slender fingers were raised and pointed toward me. The pain in my chest exploded as she neared me and I bellowed and twisted from the knife-like stabbing in my chest. I begged for the ripping and tearing to cease.

Her eyes shifted, and her hand dropped, the edge of the pain falling away. I exhaled and my eyes caught sight of a stone around her neck. Held by a leather cord, the stone was turquoise and huge. It looked too big for her slender body to carry, and it seemed to speak to me as it shimmered. Then the view of the woman was gone, barreled down by an attack from my mother.

"Leave my son alone! Leave him!"

I rolled onto my good knee and reached for the bow and quiver. My mother desperately hit the caped woman. Half kneeling, half lying down, I set an arrow in the bow and pulled back.

"Mother!"

My mother turned to me, shifting away from the fight, and I shot the arrow. The robed woman scratched at her stomach, blood appearing around the point of the arrow. I dropped to the ground, splayed from exhaustion. We stared, my mother and I, until the soldier started scrambling up the hill, the arrow still stuck in his shoulder.

"How dare you!" he screeched. His voice was high-pitched and laced with hysteria. "How-dare-you."

He stumbled, then picked himself up again. He was a boy. Not exactly a boy, but he was too young to be in an army, a young teenager probably. I felt a rush of guilt. I shot a boy. He stumbled toward us, a deranged, injured child.

"Come here," I said, reaching for my mother. She ran toward me, taking my hand.

The woman moaned out of what sounded like frustration. She held the stone necklace in her fist, clutching it like it was life itself. Red smudged the smooth turquoise surface where her bloody fingers lay. With my arms, I pushed my body halfway up until my mother helped me the rest of the way. My mother's eyes stayed locked on the dying woman.

"We must ... leave," I said between gasps of air. Her head turned from the woman and toward the battlefield.

"But your father!" she shouted.

"Mother. Now."

I urged her with an arm yank as the soldier fell to his knees. We turned and limped off the battlefield, turning back every now and then to make sure we weren't being followed.

***

"I think she's finally asleep," Rebekah whispered. She knelt next to mother's bed while I sat in a chair in the corner of the room.

I stared at my mother, an unmoving lump under the quilted blanket. Her breaths rose and fell in a steady pattern, a sure sign that she was asleep.

"You need to lie down," Rebekah said.

I didn't argue with my sister. She was right, but I kept thinking, what if she wakes up and wanders off again?

"I'll sleep in here with her," she said as if she knew my thoughts.

I nodded, bringing a hand up to my chest to feel the erratic, labored beating of my heart. I didn't tell Rebekah about the woman in the cloak. She knew we saw a soldier, but mother was so hysterical I couldn't think of a good reason to give Rebekah all of the details.

"I'm getting you a drink of water." Rebekah stood, pulling herself up by one of the bed posts. Her footsteps stopped just inside the hallway kitchen. "Knox," she called.

The tone of her voice caught my attention. I jumped up in the quickest way I could with the pulsing in my knee and pushed past the half-open bedroom door. Rebekah was standing beside the window, her back against the wall.

"Warwick soldiers," she breathed.

A dark figure moved past the window. My skin shivered and the hair on my arms stood on end.

"I knew I shouldn't have told Marc to stay at home!" Rebekah said, her voice a panicked whisper.

"Shhhh." I put my hand on her mouth.

A candle burned in my mother's bedroom. The light shone just through the crack in the door.

"Blow that out," I whispered.

Rebekah obeyed and returned to my side as I peered out the window. Three Warwick soldiers aimlessly walked our street.

"Are they looking for you?" Rebekah asked. "Maybe we should make a run for it. We could go back to my house and get Marc and Johnny and then we can leave town."

I didn't know for sure if they were looking for me. If they were, they wanted to keep me just where I was. That night the soldiers just stood keeping guard. They never banged down our door or pillaged any homes. They just watched. I knew we would never be able to escape Bear Gap. If there were three soldiers on our street, then there were three on every street.

I turned to look at Rebekah. "We have to stay here tonight." I saw tears forming in her eyes. She wanted her husband and her son, but I knew there was no way we could get to them.

Rebekah's eyes flew to the window. She gasped, pushing past me to put her hands on the sill. "Look!"

Past our dark town, on the edge of the forest, blazed a fire big enough that it turned our faces a flickering orange color.

"Is that coming from the field?" she asked.

In all my pain, I couldn't stand the sight of my sister's tears. I reached out my arm to place it around her shoulder.

"What are they doing?" she asked in horror, turning away from the scene to look at my face.

"They are burning the dead."

This is why that young soldier was out there. He was given the arduous task of pulling all of the enemy's dead bodies into piles and setting them on fire. It was an ancient war tradition in Elmyra. I say ancient because our country hadn't been in a war in hundreds of years. It told the losing party that even in defeat there was no respect. Quinten Warwick didn't allow us to gather and bury our dead. He didn't allow us a few final moments with the bodies of our loved ones. It also meant that they'd found the bodies of the caped woman and the soldier. I felt a shiver of fear for the safety of my family and myself.

My parents' home felt like an ominous, hollow haze had fallen between its walls. Rebekah's face was already red; I knew she had been crying all day, but somehow she managed to cry even more. I felt hollow myself. Like I was not me, but another person suffering through the loss of a father and the near loss of a mother. With the quietness, my physical pain became dull and emotion fell on me, like a steady rain. I turned to Rebekah and began to weep. She held me like I was her child and I felt like a child.

"I have to see Belle," I said.

"You'll see her."

"Someone has to tell her ..." An air bubble stuck in my throat. "That her husband is dead." I sounded hysterical and I could tell it worried Rebekah.

"Knox. That is not why you want to see her." Rebekah spoke through her own tears.

She was right. My sister always knew me well, too well. She knew that I needed Belle when I was feeling sad or lonely or pensive about my life. She knew my habits.

"I—I've got to tell her." I sniffled and stuttered, unable to control my own speech. I felt the slurring return.

"Knox. Listen to me." Rebekah reached down and lifted my chin. Not motherly like you may think, but abruptly. "We're going to be all right. You will see Belle again." Tears streamed down Rebekah's cheeks. "And I believe that I will see Marc again."

"And father?"

Rebekah had no answer for that. I pulled her back into a hug. We held each other for a few more minutes until breaking apart and turning back to the orange blaze.

"With the bodies gone, it'll be like the battle never happened," my sister said.

She was right. Never being able to see the body of someone you loved was torture. We would be left with a permanent question, a loose strand that could never be sewn back together or cut off. The Battle of Bear Gap would soon be a wisp of a memory to many people. To me, it would shape and mold my character for years to come.

CHAPTER FIVE

TWO DAYS LATER I was able to leave my parents' house. It took me that long to be able to stand up without yelping. Although I was nowhere close to being *better*, everything on my body did seem to be healing, everything except for my heart. I couldn't stop thinking about the cloaked woman, her sharp eyes, the turquoise stone hanging from her neck. From the moment her hand fell away, the pain in my chest, the erratic heartbeats, had been the same. Something had ripped or stretched or broken inside my chest. I found myself reaching up to steady my heart often.

"I'm going out today," I said, pulling my shirt over my head.

Rebekah was kneeling next to my mother, a plate of food in her hand.

"Are you going to your house?" she asked.

I hesitated. "Yes."

"Will you stop in town and get mother some of that mint tea that she likes? Would you like that?" Rebekah turned to speak to our mother, but there was no reply. "I have some money." She turned back to face me.

Rebekah reached into her dress and placed three rings in my hand. I rubbed my thumb over the cool, smooth surface of the money rings and then placed them in my pocket.

"It shouldn't cost that much, but take it just in case."

I nodded.

"What about the soldiers?" she asked.

Since the battle, Warwick soldiers lingered all over town. They had still made no action. They were just ... there.

"I may be the only survivor," I said. "I think he's made his point. Quinten probably doesn't care that I still live."

Rebekah nodded, only half-believing what I said. "When are you coming back?"

"I'll be back."

Before heading out the door, I took a few hobbled steps over to my mother and kissed her on her head. Rebekah had sat my mother up in my father's blue chair and wrapped a quilted blanket tightly around her lap and legs. She was still in her sleeping clothes, as she had been the previous two days. My mother was not my mother. She wouldn't speak. She wouldn't respond to anything we said. She barely ate. I wouldn't say she was empty because I watched her eyes, which still followed a person's movement or stared aimlessly as Johnny played on the floor. As of yesterday, Marc determined it was safe enough to come here and check on his wife. He'd brought Johnny over since Rebekah wouldn't leave my mother's side.

No, she wasn't empty, but she was heartbroken. So heartbroken that she just couldn't interact. So much of her internal energy was being used to mourn my father that she had none left to dress or wash herself. There was a very small part of me that was thankful for her silence. It meant not having to explain the strange events from two nights ago.

Marc sat at the kitchen table, trimming the wicks off a pile of candles, a task Rebekah had set him to. Meticulously, he cut the singed thread of each candle. The thought of Marc on the battlefield ran through my head a lot. I would have liked to see how he would have fared.

"Have another bite, Mother," Rebekah said as I opened the door to leave.

***

If a stranger had entered our town that day, he might not think anything was amiss. All the stores were open, including the street carts. Women passed through the streets with baskets of dirty clothes on their heads, heading down to the river to do their wash. Even kids bustled about, chasing their playmates and sticking crickets on little girls' shoulders. But there was a mood in our streets. There were now leering eyes instead of friendly gazes. Men doubled back and looked over their shoulders at the slightest odd noise. I found myself glancing in the direction of the battlefield and I know I wasn't the only one. Quinten and the rest of his men were still camped a mile from the center of town. No one dared to run, to flee, or to do anything out of the ordinary because this man was our new Supreme Ruler. He was now making decisions that affected our lives and everyone there had seen what happened when you rebel.

Getting the tea for my mother was not an inconvenience because I was planning on walking through town anyway. I didn't have any particular plans to go back to my house. I had planned on seeing Belle.

Belle lived on the far side of our village, out of the streets, away from the people. It was a good twenty-five-minute walk to Belle's home, and by the time I got there, my knee was stiff and blazing with pain. Belle owned a stately brick house that used to be owned by her father. When Belle and I were teenagers, her father wanted to move to the capital city, LilyAye. He was a scholarly man and preferred resources that a bigger city had. Belle didn't want that. So he stayed in Bear Gap until she was married. After he left, the house became hers, along with shelves of printed works that he collected through the years.

I felt for the small book that I always kept in my pocket. Pulling it out quickly, I opened the pages just to glance at the blue flower before closing it up and putting it back in my pocket. The book was one of Belle's that she had lent me to read. I hadn't formed the courage to return it to her yet.

A cobblestone pathway led to Belle's front door. I took the path, tucking in my shirt before shaking the brass door knocker. She didn't answer. I knocked again, reaching down to rub some of the pain out of my knee. My nerves were on edge. What if she was in danger? What if she had returned to the battlefield to look for her husband, like my mother did? I tried the door knob and it clicked open. Belle was not stupid; she would not have left her door unlocked on purpose.

"Belle!" I shouted through the high ceiling. "It's me, Knox."

Steps echoed throughout the house. I looked up to the second, third, and fourth floors, which were exposed by balconies in the cathedral ceiling.

"Belle!"

"I'm here!" she shouted back.

I physically sighed as I began pacing the length of her front hall.

"What are you doing?" I asked as she bustled through the back shelves.

"What do you mean?"

I took a few long steps to meet her. Her sandy blonde hair was pulled back into a bun, but a few strands had fallen across her face and shoulders.

"Your door was unlocked."

Her face was flushed, exasperated. "I know. Malcolm is coming by to pick up his children soon. Where's Neil?" Her eyes darted past my broad shoulders, searching for her husband.

"You're looking after Malcolm's children?" I asked, a hint of irritation in my voice that I am sure didn't go unnoticed by Belle.

"Yes." She let out a long, annoyed breath. "How's Neil? I heard the Warwicks were camped outside of town. Were you hulled up at your father's house or something? I've been stuck in here for two days. The only adult I've seen is Malcolm." Belle brushed a wisp of hair behind her ear.

"It's good that you didn't come into town."

"Neil made me promise not to leave the house until he was back." A child's squeal drifted down from one of the upstairs bedrooms. "Your knee!"

I'd forgotten about my knee for those few moments. Being with Belle, sometimes that happened. I fought the urge to tell her it was no big deal, that it barely hurt. Which would have been an awful and obvious lie because just standing in her lobby took everything in me not to moan in pain.

"My knee," I confirmed. "Let's sit down."

"All right ..." she clasped her hands together. "Let's sit." Belle's eyes left my face and her mood seemed to fall. She knew.

She led me to two curved stuffed chairs that were probably very elegant and expensive in her father's day, but now were dusty and threadbare. Neil. I needed to focus on Neil. I needed to tell Belle that her husband was dead; he was gone. It was hard for me to look at Belle, to look at her soft lips and tell her something that would crush her, and change her life. All Belle ever wanted in life was to be married and I had to tell her that she wasn't anymore.

"Knox?" She reached out to touch my hand, which was balled up in a fist on the armrest. It wasn't an affectionate touch, just a "what are you thinking?" touch. I pulled my eyes up from the floor to look at her full in the face.

"Where is Neil?"

My lips were tight and it felt like the skin on my face was turning into tree bark with all the matching grooves and wrinkles. "Gone."

It was all I could get out of my mouth. Why couldn't I have said something more comforting? Why couldn't I have said it softer, gentler? Belle was a strong woman, Neil had said so. Her light touch left my knuckles and she brought her hand to her mouth. Her eyes fell to her lap, and when she pulled her hand away from her mouth, she just stared.

"I'm sorry," I said.

"Are you sure?"

I nodded.

"Because maybe he was just taken prisoner." The skin on her chest and neck started to fill with red splotches and her breathing began to quicken.

"I don't think so."

Her eyes flashed at me. "Maybe he got away and he's hiding somewhere!" Belle's voice broke. She took shallow gasps and her body contorted so that she slumped forward, staring at her hands. Each time her lungs drew in more air, her breaths became faster and faster. Soon she was wheezing uncontrollably.

"Belle?"

She swallowed hard.

"Hey, you need to calm down." I lifted her chin so that she could look at my face.

"Do you know for certain that he's dead? Did you see him die?" The heaving steadied slightly.

"No, but I haven't seen anyone else from the battle since it happened. We were outnumbered, Belle. We had no chance."

Belle sucked in a gulp of air and lost her efforts not to cry. It was like all the heavy breathing morphed into uncontrollable crying. I watched helplessly as she rubbed the ring on her left hand. She then moved to touch the small swell of her stomach. Bringing my hand to the back of my head, I scratched at an itch that didn't exist.

"Oh, Knox ..." The flat of her hand touched her mouth and she wept quietly. "Peter?"

"Gone."

"Who will run Lindon Place?"

I just shook my head. Belle sank a little further into her chair, her body relaxing as she comprehended what I told her.

"Your father."

She didn't say it as a question. She said it more as a dawning. Like she had just remembered that she left a tea kettle on the fire.

"He died. Quinten had the bodies burned. I wasn't able to even see him. I'll never see him again, I suppose."

Bowing her head a second time, another wave of grief washed over Belle. I stared at the side of her face, her ear, her cheek, the curve or her jaw. This was real. This was my life. Everything was about to change in our territory and we all knew it. I had no father. I had no Duffy Rebellion, which had been my crusade for so long, and worse, I didn't have Belle. As if my arm were not my own, I reached out and touched Belle's elbow. She shivered at my touch, then squeezed my hand in hers.

"My mother ..." I said, my voice choking. "She hasn't spoken since."

Belle's eyes widened with my every word. They had already turned puffy and red.

"She won't eat. She barely looks at me and Rebekah."

"I'm so sorry, Knox. I—I—I know how lonely it feels." Belle's eyes were soft. I always became someone different around her. I became softer.

"I'm so sorry, Knox," she said again. "Your mother will get better. I have faith that she will."

"I wish I had died with the rest of them." My voice was so low I almost couldn't hear my own words.

"Maybe he's not dead." Belle's eyes were bright and glossy with tears. "You said you never saw your father's body. Maybe he escaped. Maybe he's alive and hiding somewhere. Maybe Neil is with him."

The battle played back in my head. When I awoke, my wounds were crudely bandaged and I had been placed safely away from the fight. How had that happened with Quinten there? He would have never let me or my father live, but I was certain that Quinten was still alive.

"I don't think so." My tone was still faint.

I reached my other hand out and placed it on the arm rest of Belle's chair. I let myself fall to the floor, settling on my good knee. Belle was short, all her features petite. So even on my knee, we were almost at eye level. Her eyes flared with worry until she let go of my hand and reached her arms out, pulling me into a warm hug. I buried myself in the comfort of *her*.

Belle had fallen from my grasp once before. I remember those months clearly when Neil was courting Belle. Then came the excruciating pain of watching them marry. I was not letting her go this time.

"Please come back to me," I whispered. My calloused fingers brushed fresh tears from my eyes.

Her body tightened. She pushed me off her.

"What did you say?"

"I want you back," I said with slightly more confidence. "I don't care about what was said in the past or that you're pregnant with Neil's child. I don't care about any of that." I moved in closer. "This could be our second chance."

Belle's face took on a look that resembled horror. "Maybe I don't want you back."

CHAPTER SIX

A SMALL VOICE shouted through the layers of Belle's house. "Mirabelle. Mirabelle," came a droning, annoying voice.

"Tuor, sweetie, I'm over here."

Belle stood, brushing the wrinkles out of her apron. I stood a moment later, staggering back a few paces to steady myself. A boy ran between us with short, quick steps. He looked about seven years old and was thin, wiry. He fell into Belle's stomach, looking up at her while wrapping his arms around her waist.

"Mirabelle," he whined.

"Where is your sister?" Belle asked.

"Upstairs."

"What's wrong?"

"She keeps taking my animals."

"Sweetie ..." Belle placed a hand on the boy's head. "You need to share. You're older, remember? You need to show Camilla how to behave properly."

"Mirabelle ..."

"Call me Aunt Mirabelle," she scolded.

Tuor caught a glimpse of Belle's splotchy face. "You look sad," he said.

"Don't you worry about that."

Tuor hesitated, staring as she continued to wipe away stray tears.

"Now go back upstairs and play."

Belle peeled away the boy's arms, pushing him in the direction of the stairs.

"But she keeps taking my animals!"

"Go!"

Tuor turned back around. With every step he took away from us, he pounded his foot hard into the floor.

"Do not stomp your feet at me!" Belle scolded. He stomped, then ran out of the room with the same flurry that he came in with.

Belle rubbed her forehead and tucked loose hairs behind her ears.

"Aunt Mirabelle?" I asked.

"I don't want them just calling me Mirabelle. I'm trying to teach them respect."

"You're not their aunt."

Belle paused, brushing her face as if to clear away any sign of grief.

"I think of them as my own children." Her voice was stern.

That was the problem. Belle always treated Tuor and Camilla like they were her own children, but they weren't.

"I'm the one who found them begging for rings," Belle continued. "I'm probably the only person they get love from." She turned to face me, placing both hands on her hips. "I don't think it's a stretch to ask them to call me 'aunt'."

It was selfish, but it bothered me when they spent time at Mirabelle's house. Tuor and Camilla took so much of Belle's attention. I wanted that attention for myself.

"Those kids need someone." I heard tears threatening in her voice again. "Portia left them when they were practically babies."

"Portia?" I asked.

"Their mother."

"Just because their mother left them doesn't mean they are your responsibility."

"I don't think of them as a responsibility! They need me now more than normal." Belle smoothed her apron out with her hands, then returned them to her hips. "That woman married Malcolm young, too young. She had Tuor and Camilla, one right after another, and then she just didn't want to be a mother anymore."

I remembered how upset Belle was when all of that happened, but it had been three years since Portia left Bear Gap. Throughout those three years, Belle spent more and more time with the children.

"Then she just left one night," Belle continued. "I'm not sure Malcolm had ever even held one of his children before Portia ran away. Now she's back in town, but she won't even see Tuor or Camilla."

"She's back?"

"She comes back sometimes," Belle said, dropping her hands from her hips and brushing past me to sit back down. My head tilted. Belle noticed my confusion. "I don't know why she does it. She just comes back occasionally and she'll only see Malcolm. Malcolm will drop everything to see her, so what am I going to do, let him leave those two home by themselves?"

A thumping came at Belle's door. She looked at me with her eyebrows scrunched together. Then the sound came again, like someone was fiddling with the handle but couldn't quite turn the knob.

"I'll get it," I said.

I touched the small knife that hung on my belt. Cautiously, my hand hovered over the knob and then I pulled the door open. A tall, burly man stood at the threshold, his body slumped over, his eyes droopy and unable to focus on me.

"Malcolm," Belle said, now at my side.

"I want my kids." Malcolm pushed through the door past Belle and me.

"Malcolm, what's wrong?" Belle asked slowly.

"Where are my kids?" he shouted. Malcolm wandered into the front hall. "Tuor!" His words came slow and slurred. "Camilla!"

"Is he hurt?" Belle asked.

I folded my arms across my chest. "No, he's drunk."

Belle looked at me as if she didn't believe what I said. "Malcolm." She tried again to get his attention.

Malcolm turned toward us, his eyes were watery. "I don't want my kids over here anymore."

"Why not?"

Malcolm sauntered toward us and I took a step closer to Belle.

"I can't work anymore!" he proclaimed. "There's no mother to watch them while I work. They need to be in the streets begging so that we have money!"

"I'll watch them while you work. That's how we've always done it." Belle's voice was quiet but hopeful. "You don't have to put them back out on the streets."

"No, no, no." Malcolm whipped his head back and forth. "Those kids are mine! I'll do what I want with them!"

"Malcolm, please." Belle walked toward him, gently placing a hand on his arm.

"Belle," I warned. The muscles in my arms tightened.

"Don't put them back out on the street," Belle pleaded. "Did something happen with Portia?"

Malcolm's eyes flashed with fury. He drew his thick forearm up and hit Belle with the back of his hand. I pounced, forgetting about the pain in my knee. Malcolm may have been bigger than me, and he may have been intoxicated, but he didn't have my rage. I wrapped my arm around his neck, pulling him down, immobilizing him. I dragged him out the front door, kneeing him in the face before throwing him down the front walkway. My leg jerked so that I almost kicked him in the stomach, but I stopped myself. His nose gushed with blood. Like the pathetic person he was, Malcolm glanced at me, then stumbled off without a word.

I was fuming. I slammed Belle's front door when I walked back inside. She was sitting, a hand to her cheek, crying.

"Do you see?" I shouted, pointing to the front door.

Belle looked up, sniffling.

"This is why you shouldn't be bothering yourself with those kids!"

"What?" Belle's voice was full of shock and malice.

"One of these days, he's going to come in here like that and I won't be here to stop him!"

Suddenly, her tears stopped and her face became very stern. "He's never done that before."

"And he won't do it again because you are done with that family."

"Excuse me?" Belle stood from her chair, dropping her hand from her cheek, which revealed a growing bruise. She took a poignant step toward me. "You are not in control of me and you will not tell me what I will or will not do."

"No, but I should be!"

"In my eyes, Malcolm Crim and Knox Duffy are not that different."

I scoffed.

"You're both bitter men that blame someone else for their problems." Belle held a finger toward the front door. "Now get out!"

**

Belle chose Tuor and Camilla over me. We had been through so much, Belle and I, yet she picked them. I had to admit that there was a small ache in my mind when I thought about those two children. I knew they were the opposite of lucky, having to be raised by a man like Malcolm. I still couldn't understand it though.

On my walk back through town, one of Quinten's soldiers rode past me, a rolled up piece of parchment under his arm. He stopped at the tree that sat in the center of town, the oldest tree in the territory was how the legend went. The soldier took a nail and posted the parchment to the thick trunk. It announced official Warwick business. Quinten would be giving a speech in the town square tomorrow and all were to attend.

CHAPTER SEVEN

"EAT SOMETHING, MOTHER," Rebekah begged. She dropped the spoon into the bowl, an act of frustration.

My parents' house was warm with Rebekah's cooking, but the smell didn't bring me the comfort that it usually did.

"Why won't you help me?" she asked.

Her head whirled around to focus on me. The days since the battle had wearied her. Rebekah's face was drawn and it seemed like new wrinkles had appeared under her eyes. I sat, unmoving. My body felt pinned to the chair by large boulders. Disgusted with myself, I turned to look away from my sister. I couldn't stop thinking about Quinten's speech tomorrow. The only thing on my mind right now was revenge.

A breeze blew against the house, causing the log-built walls to creak and moan. Johnny looked up at the sound. He sat cross-legged on the floor, a carved, wooden horse in his hand that I had made him for his last birthday. I suspected that Rebekah hoped the sight of Johnny would cheer our mother up.

"What's wrong with Grams?" Johnny asked. He left the floor to climb into my lap. I flinched when he used my knee to pull himself up.

"She doesn't feel well."

Johnny stared at my mother for many long moments. Without taking his eyes away from her, he curled up in my arm but kept his head up and alert. With Rebekah looking after our mother, Johnny's life was equally as disrupted as mine was.

"Do you want some tea?" Rebekah asked my mother. "I had Knox pick up some fresh mint leaves. I can make a mug of hot mint tea for you, your favorite."

"Where's Grandpa?" Johnny asked. His voice was quiet but still seemed to split through the room.

Rebekah's ears piqued and her shoulders rose as she drew in a deep breath. She had already explained my father's death to Johnny several times. Something in his small child's mind seemed unable to accept the passing of his grandpa. Rebekah set the bowl of broth on the small table next to my mother and crossed the room. She knelt in front of Johnny, eye level with him.

"Grandpa is gone," Rebekah said.

Her eyes were saggy and shadowed as she held her son's gaze. Johnny didn't react. He looked away from his mother and back to his wooden horse, fiddling with the hooves on the front legs.

"John," my mother mumbled from across the room. "I want my John."

My mother had started speaking that day, but the only words that came out of her mouth were about my father. They were just mumblings about a dead man.

She had become like the crazy person on the street with no home, sputtering nonsense to passersby.

"I know, Mother," Rebekah said.

Pulling herself up, she stepped toward my mother, stroked her head, then cleared the bowl away, and headed back to the kitchen. Johnny looked up to stare at my mother, a little bit of fear mixed with confusion. Back in the kitchen, Marc stood astutely watching over us. Coward, I thought as he lingered at the threshold.

"I want you to take Johnny home," Rebekah instructed Marc. "I don't want him seeing any more of this."

"John ..." my mother mumbled.

Johnny curled up tighter in my lap.

"We only arrived yesterday." Marc stepped over to set a cup down on the table, a little harder than normal.

"I know. I just don't want Johnny to get this image of my mother like this." Rebekah's voice was quiet to keep the discussion private, but we could hear it well.

"Maybe he needs to see it. She may never go back to normal."

His words were not angry, just matter of fact. There was a marked silence in the kitchen. Rebekah didn't respond. My mother didn't say anything and Johnny didn't move, not even the usual squirm of a seven-year-old. Another gust of wind hugged the walls of the house.

"It's just the truth," Marc said. "I've seen this happen to people. Their head never returns to the state it was in before. Maybe this is good for Johnny."

"Do you know how hard this is for me?" Rebekah's voice dropped to almost a whisper. Tears threatened. The lilt in her voice gave her away.

"It's hard for me too. I have to constantly explain to Johnny why his mother is not home or why he can't see your father."

My hand clawed at the wood grain of the chair I was sitting in. Don't move, I told myself. Just don't get involved.

"Johnny."

It was my mother that spoke. Her droning had turned to something clear. My eyes snapped up and she looked right at me, right at Johnny.

"Come here, boy," she said, her eyes bright.

Johnny sat up straight in my lap.

"Grams!"

His face beamed and he stumbled off my lap and up onto my mother's. She took him, wrapping her thin arms around him. I moved to the edge of my chair, watching carefully. For a moment, a smile began to form on my face as my mother kissed Johnny on the top of his head.

The boy had been named after my father. It was nontraditional, but Rebekah had such a hard time being pregnant with Johnny that she thought she wouldn't have any other children. She begged Marc to let her name their son John instead of Marc.

"Just go," Rebekah said, her voice pulling my attention back to the kitchen.

Marc slid past Rebekah. His boots clicked across the wood floor as he took long strides toward my mother.

"It's time to go home, son."

"No! Father, I want to stay with Grams."

All I wanted to do was shout, stop! STOP! I stood from my chair, my heart thumping the quick beats I had become accustomed to.

"Let's go," Marc said.

His voice never rose in pitch. Wearily, he tried to slip his arm around Johnny to pull him off my mother's lap, but Johnny held on.

"Noooo," Johnny whined.

"Mother?" Rebekah was next to me, watching my mother with an open mouth.

Tears came to my mother's eyes. Not the terrible weeping from the day my father died but gentle tears. She held Johnny tight to her breast.

"Son, it's time to leave. Come away from your Grams."

"Marc, wait," Rebekah said.

Marc sighed and shifted his body out of awkward frustration. Slowly, I brought my hand to my chest. Focus on the beating, I told myself. I tried not to think about what a brute Marc was being.

"Mother, are you feeling better?" Rebekah asked, taking careful steps toward her.

"I want my John back."

"My John." That's what mother always boasted was her nickname for our father. In that moment, my mother was back in her delusion.

"Would you still like me to take our son home?" Marc asked.

His face was calm. His eyes lacked the mystery that mine and Rebekah's held. My sister's face turned livid. Her patience snapped like a twig.

"Have you no senses?" she shouted. "Can't you see my mother is embracing our child?"

Rebekah threw both her hands up and pounded on Marc's chest. He took the blows as if they came from anywhere but his own wife.

"You just asked me to take him home. I am only doing what *you* asked me to do."

"You act like you don't even care about our family," she said, dropping both arms to her side. "You wouldn't even stand and fight with my father."

I could tell they were words Rebekah wanted to say for a long time but had held back in support of her husband.

"If I had, I'd likely be dead. I won't apologize for not leaving you a widow." Marc shifted away from us, his face toward the door. "You are not acting like yourself," he said, quickly turning to face us again. "Your father is gone, but your husband and your son are still alive and we need you."

My ears started to feel like they were filling up with water. Marc tried to reach down to pick up Johnny again, determined to obey my sister's wishes and take him home. I couldn't take the sight of him reaching his greedy, uncaring hands out one more time, and I, too, tumbled out of control. There were two steps between me and Marc. I took them in one long stride. Pushing Rebekah out of the way, I punched Marc hard in the jaw.

It was an instant release. He stumbled back until he collapsed on the floor. I stepped forward again, taking the collar of his shirt in my hand and drew back to punch him again.

"Knox!"

Rebekah screamed, scratching at my arm to stop the blow to her husband. I barely noticed her. I hit Marc again. Blood appeared under his nose and his face turned a blotchy blue. This is nothing, I thought, nothing compared to what my father went through.

Rebekah was in front of me then, her hands pushing and shoving me off her husband. I dropped my grip so that Marc's head fell flat on the floor. His eyes swam. Rebekah took his head in her lap. I turned back only for a moment to look at my mother and Johnny, the old and the young, neither in a mindset to understand what had just taken place. Then I left swiftly, because Rebekah had a fury in her eyes that matched mine.

I walked a quarter of a mile into the woods before I started to notice the pain in my hand. The trees that surrounded me were like my buffer against the rest of the world. I shouted and cursed into the branches above me, the urge to hit something still coursing through me. I sat down on the forest floor, letting my anger drip away at the pace that grass grows. My knuckles were speckled with Marc's blood. I had hurt a member of my family. That was something I wasn't proud of. So I needed a new enemy. I had always disliked Marc, but I had never hurt him before that day. None of this would have happened if it weren't for—

"Quinten."

I said his name out loud. He was the reason I hit Marc, because he was the reason Rebekah was neglecting her family, because he was the reason my mother had been catatonic, because he was the reason my father was dead.

Finally, my breathing evened. It was time for me to return to my home. I lived in the swamps, an area of Bear Gap the poor were known to call home. I didn't mind it. It was in the woods, away from the bustle of the town.

When I opened the door to my home, it struck me as odd. The walls, the floors, the furniture, they were all a part of my life when my father was alive. Now I had to return and it felt like I needed to inform all my belongings of the bad news: Quinten had ruined my life.

Before falling asleep, I made a decision, a plan. I was set on my plan. I slept that night with my clothes on and blood still dried on my hand.

CHAPTER EIGHT

I DIDN'T WASH or change my clothes the next morning. I guzzled down a cup of stale water and chose to be hungry instead of picking at the rotten apple on my table. I was in the town square early, ready for Quinten's speech. The square was busy, and even as the crowd began to thicken, I paced with my arms folded, seething like a sick animal. Villagers gawked at me. Was it my unsteady limp? My habit of clutching at my chest? Or my bloody hand that caused them to stare?

A platform had been built in an open space behind the posting tree. Four or five soldiers lined the back of the platform and a few other soldiers were planted among the crowd. Soon the village square was full. I glanced up at the burning sun.

Behind me someone shouted instructions. "Move in! Everybody move up. Go on, push in closer."

Warwick soldiers herded everyone together until people pressed on me from all sides. Moments later, Quinten arrived on his horse, forcing the crowd to part in order to let him through. He waved modestly while a trail of guards on horseback protected him on all sides. Quinten dismounted. The clank of his boot buckles spread through the air as he approached the platform. He smiled into the warm air. The sun blinked at the red W embroidered on his black vest.

"I thank each of you for your kind welcome into my territory," he began. His voice echoed across the tops of our heads. "It has been an honor to get to know these lands and to learn your culture. As you know, Bear Gap is my southernmost territory." Quinten let out a light chuckle. "Let me tell you, things are done quite differently here than they are up north, where I was born." He lifted his chin and looked above the crowd for a moment. "My campaign as Supreme Ruler is simple; you'll have more help from me and my council so that you can prosper and live better lives." It seemed incredible to me how different this person was from the one I met on the battlefield.

"Hunger and poverty are rampant in parts of our kingdom and your old Supreme Ruler turned away from it. For months, I have been traveling our nation and I cannot ignore this problem anymore. I see the worried looks on some of your faces. I need you to understand something.

"One of the first things my advisors told me when I become Supreme Ruler was that there was a problem with the seed. That's right, the seed. Now, I don't understand all the details, but my scientists tell me that our seed—our wheat seed, our barley seed, our corn seed—they're all becoming infected." Quinten looked firmly at the crowd as he placed a fist into the palm of his other hand.

"Disease is spreading throughout our crops and if it hasn't yet made it here to Bear Gap, it will. No one was doing anything about it, until now. Next spring, I will be implementing a nationwide program. I know there have already been rumors flying around the territories, and I'm here to set those rumors straight. A standard national farm will be developed that will provide food for the whole kingdom." Quinten flashed a bright smile and the crowd clapped, reluctantly at first and then the applause picked up as Quinten allowed an uncomfortable amount of silence to settle.

"So, for the next several months, we will be collecting all seeds and destroying them so that the good seed, which my scientists are holding back in LilyAye, can be used to start a new crop next spring. This new farm ..."

Quinten leaned his face in closer. "I will be starting this farm right here in Bear Gap." There were several moments of silence before the crowd erupted in applause. I stood staunchly with my arms folded across my chest. "This farm will supply food for the rest of our kingdom and provide jobs for the citizens of this territory. Bear Gap is a rural, secluded corner of Elmyra that I want to turn into a prospering town with lots of opportunity. Elmyra has a total of six territories under my rule and that doesn't include LilyAye, which has the highest population. Down here, you folks have the longest summers and the greatest number of days to grow crops. Each one of you will be instrumental in providing nourishment to the rest of the country." Quinten held his lips tightly together and thought for a moment before continuing.

"I want to address something before I step down." His eyes turned big and glossy. "An uncomfortable event took place just outside your town a few days ago." I felt my chest tighten. "There are those that question my authority as Supreme Ruler, but worse than that, there are those that wish to stop progress. It was an unfortunate thing that took place, but as Supreme Ruler, I don't just think about one person. I think about our whole nation. I have to decide what is best for the most people. "

An eerie silence floated through the crowd. I could feel my ears burning. I was going to do it. I was going to scream out and charge the stage. I wasn't far away, only a few people stood in between us. My body jerked as if I were going to run, but then my attention was pulled away from the platform.

"Liar! Liar!" A woman's scream split through the mass of people.

My head bobbed to look, but the crowd was so dense I couldn't see.

"You're a liar and a murderer!" The cries were blood-curdling. People started to whisper and mumble.

"You're a filthy liar!"

"Now, I know," Quinten said, "I know this is hard for some of you."

With the nod of Quinten's head, a Warwick soldier was deployed into the crowd. He charged through the crowd as he drug the woman away. Then there was silence again.

"I know this is hard for some of you," Quinten repeated. "But I promise you. I became Supreme Ruler because I wanted to help communities like yours." Quinten paused. "I will bring this farm to Bear Gap and I will make your territory prosperous and ... I will make it famous." Quinten stared until another round of reluctant claps started.

I looked at the other villagers. No one believed any of this, did they? People grinned and leaned in to make comments to their friend. They were engrossed and attentive, save the families that were related to Duffy Rebellion members. Who was that woman? I was certain her husband or brother were one of the men who died alongside my father. I found that I couldn't look at Quinten's face. I couldn't look at the man who was responsible for my father's death.

"Moving forward," Quinten continued, "I will start by appointing a governor to Bear Gap that will oversee this project. You will notice a lot of changes around here, but I promise each one will be for the good. Together we can feed the whole nation!"

Quinten stepped down from the platform, a silly grin on his face. He stepped away, chuckling and slapping the backs of some of his companions. A genuine mood of excitement flooded the crowd. Quinten had done exactly what he came to do. He squelched the rebellion and made everyone love him. Well, not everyone. There were a few stern faces in the crowd besides mine. I was too scared to face any of those people though, too scared they would ask me about their loved ones, or worse, blame me for their death. Then there would be the question, "How did you survive?" That was a question I couldn't answer. If only they knew how badly I wished I had died with the rest of them.

The crowd began to break up. People returned to their homes or their shops. Mothers took their children by the hand and ushered them out of the street. I stood unmoved. I felt like I could skin Quinten with my eyes. One of Quinten's men shook his hand and said, "Good job!". My disdain for him made my body quiver. All of a sudden, it felt like hot oil was being poured on my heart.

"Knox."

My body flinched. I turned around to a gentle touch on my shoulder. Belle. I let out a breath. Her skin looked pale in the sunlight and she had a little girl by the hand, Camilla.

"Hi," she said. Her eyes looked weary from crying.

I tried to pull my mind away from Quinten. Belle looked down, fiddling with the ring on her finger.

"I'm sorry about the other day." She raised her head to look at me.

I quickly tucked my hands deeper into the folds of my arms to try and hide the blood.

"I've known you my whole life, Knox. We've always been friends, and when I married Neil, I just ... I missed spending time with you. And now, I think it's hard for us to be friends again."

There was a pause. Belle brought a hand to her mouth, stifling tears. I looked down as Camilla bounced around while tethered to her arm. "I miss him so much. I'll get through it, I suppose."

"I'm sorry too," I said although I couldn't think of a single word I said that I didn't mean. I didn't want to see Belle cry though. I never wanted to see her cry.

Ahead of me was a row of houses and shops and between two homes was an alley. Tuor ran up and down the alley and then jumped up the front porch steps to one of the homes. He did this three times before the woman of the house opened the door and swatted him away with a broom.

"Tuor!" Belle shouted. "I'm sorry," she said, turning back to me.

"Where is Malcolm?" I felt the muscles in my neck tighten.

"He's here. He was here for Quinten's speech. Tuor and Camilla just found me and wanted to say hello." Belle's voice took on that tone that it did when she spoke of children. She released Camilla's hand and pulled the little girl close to her side, resting a hand on her shoulder.

"But now," she continued, covering Camilla's ear with her hand, "their mother is right over there." Belle's eyes glanced over her shoulder and then back at me. "She'll talk to Malcolm, but she won't talk to her children. It makes me sick. When the kids ran up to me, she sauntered over and pulled Malcolm to the side. I think all she does is go from one man to another."

I followed Belle's eyes toward a bakery cart a few houses down. Next to the cart stood Malcolm with the woman he used to call his wife. The back of Malcolm's massive frame shielded most of Portia's body as the two spoke.

"Why does this become your responsibility?" I asked. Without thinking I pulled my arms out of their fold. Belle's eyes grew big as she saw my beaten and bloody knuckles.

"What is going on with you?"

"Nothing." My eyes left her inquisitive face and I focused on the back of Malcolm's head. "It's nothing," I repeated.

"What happened! Why are your hands bloody?"

Malcolm shifted on his feet and it was like a curtain was drawn back. He revealed a woman, slender faced with green eyes and a cape shrouded over her shoulders. For a moment I stared. The form looked eerily familiar.

Lying on her chest was a turquoise stone. My breath caught in my throat and suddenly my stomach felt sour. She was the woman from the battlefield. Instinctively, my hand found contact with my chest. I struggled to breathe. She was dead. I thought she was dead. She *should* have been dead.

"Knox?" Belle's hand waved in front my face. Her eyes turned to stare where I was staring.

"What's wrong?" she asked, her worried tone colored with a hint of irritation.

"Is that Portia?" I asked.

"Yes. Why?" Belle's head darted back and forth and her eyebrows furrowed.

My mouth went dry. Portia's eyes flickered past Malcolm and focused on me. She smiled at me coolly, bringing her hand up to stroke the smooth turquoise stone on her neck.

CHAPTER NINE

"KNOX?"

BELLE'S VOICE fizzled so that I almost didn't hear her calling my name. I backed away, steadying my head with my hand. Confusion coated Belle's face as she scrunched her eyebrows together. I walked away from her without an explanation, ducking between two shops on the opposite side of the street.

I watched Portia carefully, blinking my eyes over and over again just to make sure I wasn't hallucinating. She stroked Malcolm's arm tenderly, even once reaching up to touch the stubble on his cheek. When she talked it was like watching the wind catch on a flag. Her lips flowed up and down, never a move or word spoken without meaning.

How is she alive?

My mind spun with that question. Not only was she alive, but she looked ... well. She held no sign of injury. I forced myself to think back on the actions of that night. Mother had tackled her to the ground, and then I shot her. I shot her with an arrow and I saw it hit her stomach, a mortal wound. The image was branded in my memory. I looked up again. It was her. The stone around her neck made me sure.

Finally, I turned away from the scene, leaning up against the side of one of the shops. The stone wall was cool on my back. How she lived was only part of my problem. Portia saw me. What if she recognized me? She knew I tried to kill her and the soldier she was with on the battlefield. I didn't care about myself. I cared for Belle more than I did my own flesh.

Portia had to be working with Quinten. Why else would she have been on that battlefield? It wasn't just coincidence that Portia was back in town at the same time that Quinten brought his army to Bear Gap. She was on the Warwick side. In that moment it dawned on me. This was where Quinten found his power, through a woman who couldn't die. I couldn't figure out what Portia was getting out of the arrangement, but I had another realization. I now had a real reason to convince Belle to stop looking after Portia's children.

By the time I left my hiding spot, Belle was gone and most of the town square was empty. I hobbled through the streets, pushing myself as hard as I could. I caught up with Belle ambling through the field that led to her house. The grass was waist high, but there was a small path that had been worn. I paused to watch Belle for a moment. She touched the top of the grass as she walked. She didn't have the children with her, which was probably why she looked so sullen. My labored breathing and unsteady footsteps caught Belle's attention.

"What is going on?" she asked, turning around to look at me. She placed both hands on her hips.

"You don't understand." I placed my hands on my thighs, trying to catch my breath.

"Knox, you look sick." Her tone was sweet but serious.

"You can't watch Tuor and Camilla anymore."

Belle sighed and her hands dropped from her hips. "That's what this is about?"

"It's not safe!"

"Because of Malcolm? He was drunk that day. It's never happened before."

I stood up straight. "No. It's their mother—she's a part of the Warwick Army. She's on Quinten's side."

Belle's gaze intensified around me.

"She was at that battle, Belle. I saw her. She was there, helping another Warwick soldier."

"Oh, Knox ..."

I felt myself getting angry with Belle. It seemed like she didn't hear anything I was saying. "Belle, it's dangerous. Please believe me, she's a dangerous woman!"

"If this is true, then why are you only telling me now?" Belle's hands stayed firmly pressed into her hips.

"I didn't recognize her until just now."

Belle looked at me with great sympathy as if I were a dying animal. I knew she didn't believe a word I spoke.

"She has some sort of power," I said. "She did something to my heart." I laid my hand on my chest to help her understand. "It aches constantly."

"Are you saying she's... enchanted? That she's placed some sort of curse on you?"

"Yes!"

"Oh, Knox." Belle let her hands fall from her hips. "You are really struggling with your father's death. I understand. I miss Neil so much and—"

"I'm telling the truth!"

Belle took a step toward me and waited until I caught my breath. "Portia probably is running around with Quinten," she said. "She is probably doing lots of other terrible and selfish things. Portia is not a good person, Knox, and she's a horrible mother, but that's it, that's all that she is."

"Then how do you explain my heart?"

"Look at yourself! Your knee is in terrible shape, you can barely stand. You just fought in a battle and, your father's dead. Your heart is probably stressed from everything you've been through."

"You still shouldn't be helping that family."

"I don't look after Tuor and Camilla because their parents are good people. It's not Tuor and Camilla's fault that their mother is on the enemy's side."

"What if you get caught in the crosshairs? What if Portia comes by someday to take her children and she sees you breaking a new Warwick law? You heard Quinten, no more seed. We can't even grow our own crops anymore! What if she catches you using some of this supposed infected seed?"

Belle's face was soft but unyielding.

"I can't watch you have dealings with these people," I continued.

"Portia will never come to see her children. She hates her children. She blames them for her lost freedom." Belle's eyes started to water. She put a hand on her chest, just below her neck. "I could starve those children or call them my own; it makes no difference to their mother."

A breeze blew by, shaking the grass surrounding us. I shifted my weight onto my good knee and felt like I was out of arguments.

"Don't you trust me?" I asked.

Belle bowed her head and took a long, shaky breath. She drew her arms together. "I wish you wouldn't ask me that."

The death of Neil had worn on her. She claimed that Tuor and Camilla needed her, but I could now see that she really needed them.

"You used to trust me," I said, searching for her eyes. "You used to listen to anything I said. I've done nothing that should change that." I felt my voice rising.

Belle tilted her head up. "That's right. You've done *nothing.*"

Her words felt like a serpent's bite, but she was right. When Neil started courting Belle, I just watched idly. I hated Neil and said a string of terrible things about him in my mind, but I never once tried to take Belle for myself. At the time I told myself I was doing the honorable thing, stepping aside so Belle could be happy. I was really just being a coward. I was too wrapped up in myself that I couldn't see what I was missing out on. I'd lost the greatest woman because of my pride.

"You didn't love him like you loved me," I said. "You married him even when you still loved me. Was that fair to Neil?"

"Nothing was fair! Nothing in this world is fair." Belle's eyes flashed with fury. A fury I'd seen so rarely. "Yes, I loved you, Knox. I loved you a great deal, but you're angry and bitter and my love has faded." She paused. "I could never marry you."

"This again?" I threw up my hands and took a half step backward.

"You're proving it right now! The smallest thing sets you off. How do I know you wouldn't do to me what you did to Malcolm?"

"I would never do that." My teeth clenched tightly together.

"What about that blood on your hands, Knox? Whose blood is that? I can't live with a man knowing that he might come home the sweet, loving man I fell in love with or the man covered with someone else's blood!"

"It's hard right now. My father just died." I grabbed for excuses.

"You were like this before your father died. You've been like this for years," Belle snapped back, keeping pace with me. "It's true, I may have never loved Neil as much as I loved you." She hung her head. "But I loved him enough and he was kind and he had a peace inside of him that you don't have." She raised her head to look me in the eye. Then placed her petite hand on my cheek. "Every time I'm with you, all I see is a storm raging in those eyes."

We stared at each other, the quiet of the field absorbing our rage.

"I'm going to kill Quinten," I said. Belle pulled her hand away. "He killed my father, Belle. He's ruining this country."

"Don't be foolish," Belle whispered.

"You are supporting it. Someday, those kids are going to get you into trouble," I said. My voice was lowered but still riddled with anger. "Because when you cook with poison, you make yourself sick. When you get sick, don't come to me for help."

I hobbled away, determined never to bother myself with that woman again.

CHAPTER TEN

I WAS SO jittery from my fight with Belle that it felt like my skin was covered in ants. The scenery around Belle's house was a blur. Each step I took back to town, my heart rate quickened. I walked into the street and my head started to feel dizzy and light. My hand grabbed for the nearest building. Breathe, I told myself, breathe. My chest heaved in and out.

"You all right, boy?"

My heavy eyes looked up at an old, thin man shrouded in brown fabric. He held onto the wooden handle of a garden tool. It was his house I was clinging to. Slowly, my heart began to steady.

Belle was right, I realized. My anger had overtaken me. Every time I thought of Quinten or Portia or Marc ... or Neil ... I found myself losing control. What did Belle really want from me? Did she expect me to forget about my father? Did she expect me to let our home territory be turned into Quinten's big project? I couldn't do that. I couldn't let my father's death go unavenged.

Breathe, Knox, breathe.

"Are you all right?" the old man repeated.

"Yes." I turned my posture upright.

The old man nodded and ducked back behind his house. There was a part of me that hated conceding to Belle. I decided not to act on my anger. Belle would be furious if she knew the thoughts whirling inside my head. I imagined the different ways I could kill Quinten. Perhaps I'd ask him how he killed my father and then I could do the same to him. I decided to hold back, for Belle.

My mother and sister were on my mind, but I wasn't ready to see them. Not after what had happened with Marc. I knew I needed to apologize to him, but I wasn't ready for that either. I didn't want to go back to my empty house in the swamps, so I stopped at Lindon Place. Lindon Place was the only inn and restaurant in our village. Up until the battle, it was owned by Peter Lindon. He was now gone, burned with my father.

The inn sat on one of the corners that made up the town square. Its windows were short and dark, and when I entered the dining room, I was greeted by a heavy haze of smoke from the cracked chimney. Only a few tables were occupied. I chose a seat in a high-backed booth against the wall, rubbing the back of my neck as I sat down. A teenage girl approached my table, with straight, shiny golden hair. She was one of Peter's daughters, although I didn't know which one because he had many.

"What would you like?" she asked. She exuded politeness, but there was also something very solid about her nature. She kept her chin raised ever so slightly.

"Water."

"I can't serve you unless you buy something."

"What?" I asked blinking at her. The pain in my chest was still a sharp throb.

"You can't just sit here and drink water; you have to purchase something." She held her lips tightly together. Like me, her father had died just a few days prior and she was holding it together better than I was.

I sighed, turning in my chair to face her better. A couple sat a table away from me. They were young. I could tell they were locals, but I didn't know their names.

"What's the cook making tonight?" I tried to push my frustration away.

"Turnip and bean stew."

"Fine," I said shifting back so I couldn't see anyone.

Her feet moved away from my table in hard, steady steps. Lindon Place was a homey, rustic establishment. A door in the back led to the kitchen. Next to it stood a line of girls, all different ages, waiting to serve whoever might enter. Among the girls was one seated woman, Peter's wife, and a toddler hanging on the hem of her apron.

I closed my eyes, rubbing my temples. I tried to empty my mind, but the couple's conversation kept catching my attention. They spoke of Quinten.

"I heard said that he leaves tonight," the man said. "Tonight?"

I opened my eyes and strained to see their faces.

"Urgent matter in LilyAye." His spoon rubbed against a wooden bowl. "Apparently, a rider came just after his speech and delivered the word." He spoke through a mouthful of turnip and bean stew.

The woman shifted in her chair. "I'll be glad when he's gone," she said.

"Watch it!" The man's voice dropped. "Watch what you say around here. He's our Supreme Ruler now."

He pulled on his wife's arm and mumbled something into her ear. "Besides, I think he could do some real good around here."

The bare skin on the back of my neck prickled. My eyes made a sweep of the dining room. There were no Warwick soldiers that I could see. There was no way the Lindons were Warwick supporters. What was he so paranoid about? Had Quinten really instilled that much fear? The fire popped in the corner of the room, splaying tiny embers on the floor.

"Why does he need an army to *do good*?" the woman asked.

"Milly!"

"I don't like it."

The Lindon girl returned with my bowl of stew. She placed a spoon and a chunk of bread on the table.

"Here," she said.

There was no water. The girl turned quickly on her heels, but I called after her. "How about some water now?"

She paused for a moment, smoothing a crease in her skirt.

"Yes, I'll get that for you."

"Excuse me," I called again before she could walk away.

"Yes." She turned back to face me.

"I knew your father." I let the words hang in the air. The girl didn't respond. "I'm sorry about what happened to him. What's your name?"

"My name is Eve, sir."

"Sorry," I said again.

"Thank you." Eve turned and walked away.

My water arrived when I was nearly finished with my stew. Eve seemed slightly more affable toward me, but it was hard to tell. I pushed my empty bowl away and moved to leave, but the couple caught my ear again.

"It'll bring in more rings for people like us," the man said.

"How is that?"

"More people here workin' the farm, creatin' more business, then they spend their rings at places like this."

The woman held a mug in her hand. She pulled it across the wooden table as she contemplated her husband's words. "I suppose that's good."

"I told you to listen to me. I know what I say."

Money. This woman was convinced of Quinten because it would bring more money to Bear Gap? I felt sick. I stood quickly, hitting the bottom of my table with my leg so that the empty stew bowl rolled onto the floor. The noise caught the couple's attention.

"Do you think my father's life is worth a few extra rings?" I asked in a deep, hoarse tone. From the corner of my eye, I saw Peter's wife stand from her chair.

"What's that, sir?" the husband asked.

"My father died at the hand of Quinten Warwick and you think that that's all right because you might be a bit richer?" I took two steps closer to their table and rested my knuckles on the surface.

"Pardon?"

"We meant no offense," the wife said, rightfully concerned.

I turned my hands into fists and pounded them both on the table. The woman jumped.

"You are the reason Quinten is so powerful!" I turned to face the rest of the dining room, including all of Peter's daughters. Eve caught my eyes as she stood firm as a statue by the kitchen door. I turned back to the couple. "My father is worth more than this!"

I grabbed the edge of the table and turned in on its side. The woman's mug fell and broke on the floor and leftover stew speckled the wood planks. The couple said nothing but stared at me wide-eyed. My feet took me in a straight line to the door. I turned to get one more glimpse of Eve, who still stood unfazed. She gave me a silent look of approval, which was exactly what I needed.

The town passed by me unseen as I headed back to my home in the swamps. Throwing the door open, I tossed everything I needed into a canvas bag: a canteen of water, some eggs, a potato, my flint, a whetstone, and my small knife. I stumbled around my little cabin, knocking over the one chair I owned. Then I was gone. I tried to keep Belle far from my mind. I couldn't remember why I cared so much about a woman's opinion who wasn't even my wife.

The gate that led out of town was still hanging open. It was like an omen to anyone who stumbled upon our little town. I paused a moment before stepping into the stretch of land that would now always be a battlefield in my mind. The bodies were gone. Quinten had done a good job cleaning up his mess. There were still pools of congealed and dried blood. There were patches of matted grass and divots from horses' hooves.

I followed the fenced tree line bordering the town until the Warwick camp came into view. I stepped out of sight and into the woods, keeping my eyes set on the camp's movement. It was afternoon and Quinten planned on leaving soon. Soldiers worked intently to roll up tents, load the wagons and horses, and stamp out the fires.

It took just over an hour from when I started watching for them to pack up camp and start on their way. They headed north toward LilyAye on the one road leading out of our territory. Quinten led his army, save one soldier in front of him for protection. When they started moving, I jumped up and sprinted along the edge of the woods to follow. It was a two-day journey to LilyAye. I only needed to follow until they set up camp for the night. With each jaunt I felt a stab of pain in my knee, but I ignored it.

I had to jog most of the way to keep up. The wagons forced them to go at a slow enough pace that I could manage, despite the gnawing pain in my knee. I followed through the dense woods surrounding Bear Gap. A few times I had to stop and hide behind a tree because my feet caught the attention of one of the soldiers last in line.

As the sun set, the air grew cool, and I struggled to keep up with the caravan. My lungs burned and it felt like my knee was grinding bone on bone. They continued for a while longer, using torches to light the way. Finally, the lead soldier yelled back, "Stopping!" The caravan came to a shifting halt. I darted far into the woods.

It wasn't until I sat down on a fallen tree that the pain became really intense. The rag wrapped around my knee was moist with thick blood. I hadn't brought anything to replace the bandage, not even a blanket or spare shirt. I wasn't concerned about my knee because, in my mind, there was no life for me after this night. It wasn't that I thought I would die necessarily; I just hadn't made any plans after killing Quinten. Murder was the only thing I was thinking about.

I lit a small fire, forced myself to eat one of my eggs, and then sat and waited, my leg extended in front of me to rest my knee. It was fully dark. When I thought I had waited long enough, I decided to wait longer. I pulled my knife and whetstone out of my bag and worked on sharpening the blade. It was a habit of mine. My mother liked to quilt to keep her hands busy. Rebekah was constantly clearing away dishes or offering to fill a drink. I liked to sit and sharpen my knives. Every stroke of the blade made a quiet *wsheeit* sound and I let my mind go numb with the repetitiveness of it. When my arm grew tired, I set aside the knife and whetstone in exchange for something much gentler. My hand found contact with the blue flower I kept hidden in my little book. My fingers always seemed far too rough and calloused to be handling something so delicate. Swimming with emotion, I quickly tucked the flower away. I needed to focus.

A quiet thudding noise drifted through the trees. It broke through the peaceful sound of rustling leaves and crickets that had turned dull in my brain. Every sense in my body became heightened. I stamped out my fire, now suddenly aware of how late it was and how much I didn't want to miss this opportunity. I would sneak into Quinten's tent and slit his throat. Whatever happened after that, I didn't care.

Leaving my whetstone, I kept my knife firm in my

hand and listened for the noise. It was coming in the direction of the road, a distant trotting sound. Slowly and steadily, I walked back toward the road and Quinten's camp. My hand clenched the smooth, worn handle of my knife. As I drew nearer, the road appeared, a thin clearing between the trees. The thudding sound grew closer until massive horse hooves rode into view. The moon created a blue haze as if to draw all my focus onto the person riding down the worn dirt road.

CHAPTER ELEVEN

PORTIA RODE HER horse up the empty road toward Quinten's camp. Her head was covered with the hood of her cape. I had no doubt that it was the woman whose bare hand had crippled my heart. I could tell by the sway of her body and the way her thin fingers gripped the horse's reins.

I remained still until she passed me and then I tried to follow her. Before I could take my first step, her head snapped around, searching the darkness. Her eyes looked glassy in the soft hue of moonlight. Staring into the woods, she was like a dog, sniffing out a squirrel. Then she turned and continued on, her horse creating a steady, hammering noise as it walked. I waited a few more moments before getting closer to the road and following her.

The Warwick Army had set up their camp off the road in the thick forest. Tents filled up the spaces between the trees and a few fires burned with glowing embers. Portia dismounted, pulling her hood back to reveal her pale face. The way she scanned the woods, it looked as if she could see clearly in the dark. This seemed like a habit of hers, seeking out Quinten late at night. Her cape swished past a low-burning fire. She approached one of the tents and reached down to pull back the flap when Quinten stepped out.

"Where have you been?" he asked. His voice was low and scratchy. He was wearing a loose cotton shirt and looked weary.

Portia's lips formed a crease. She looked at him as if she were doling out a punishment. Quinten pushed past Portia, turning around to look at her with a hint of disgust.

"I've barely seen you since the battle. Then I tell you we have to leave today and you're nowhere to be found." He turned to face her fully. "I can't just wait for you with my men around."

Portia followed Quinten a few paces out of the camp, but somehow I got the feeling that Quinten was following her lead.

"I told you I needed to see my children," she said.

"Your children? You mean Malcolm. I know you spent all week with him." Quinten's face crept closer to hers as if to tempt Portia. He chuckled to himself. "I ask you to do one thing, to protect my nephew, and he comes back to camp with an arrow wound."

"Yes, tell me about what truly has you upset."

"I'm surprised he's still alive. You are the most flighty woman I have ever known. You're here next to me one moment and then I'll wake the next morning and you've disappeared."

Portia's face was like a marble statue. She was cold but calm. Quinten folded his arms across his chest, waiting for an answer.

"I have made all of this possible for you, my Supreme Ruler." Portia bowed in mock respect. "If I want to go here or there when I please, I think it's a fair exchange for me helping you become ruler of this land."

Quinten chuckled again as he averted his eyes. I could tell this argument was a common refrain.

"Your nephew was berating some village woman, so her son shot him," Portia said. "I protected him. He wouldn't be alive if I hadn't been there."

My eyes flitted to Portia's necklace. The turquoise stone was so smooth that light glared off its surface. She reached up to feel the curve of the stone.

"What if he had died? My family has charged me with his care. My nephew's mind is not right. Think how my uncle will react when he sees that Reed has a scar on his shoulder." Quinten rubbed the top of his head with his hand. "I'm feeling enough pressure as Supreme Ruler, and from my family, and now I have to deal with you!"

"Quinten," Portia cooed. She reached her hand up to stroke his cheek. Quinten shied away at first but then leaned in closer. "You know what I can do. You have no need to worry. Your enemies are my enemies and no one can bring harm to us."

Portia brought her other hand around to Quinten's back as she leaned in to kiss him. Their lips met for a moment until Quinten pulled away.

"No one can do harm to *you*," he clarified. "But what about me?"

"I'm on your side."

"If you were on my side, then you would let me wear the amulet."

Portia remained calm, but her body flinched ever so slightly at the mention of her necklace.

"I'm in more danger than you," Quinten continued.

Portia took a half step away from Quinten. "You're envious of my powers. Don't let that overtake you."

"If you're on my side then why won't you help me?"

"Is this all you want me for?" Portia made a face, like she was pouting.

"No. Of course not." He reached out to pull Portia closer to him. "Come back to camp with me. Sleep here tonight and we'll ride home together tomorrow."

Portia seemed to yield for a moment but then pushed away.

"You'll never have my amulet," she whispered. Quinten's face gave a frustrated look. "I've hidden it from minds. Those who desire it will be unable to find it." The corner of Portia's mouth curled up slightly into a smile. "You can be Supreme Ruler like you wanted, but you will never get my amulet."

Portia took two marked steps away.

"Portia, please ..."

"You treat me like dirt, yell at me, and then ask to have the most precious thing I own."

"I didn't mean it like that."

Portia stroked the amulet on her chest. Quinten seemed oblivious to the stone, whereas I felt like I was being drawn to it. She turned from him, pulling her hood back up. Quinten looked like he might call out to her, but instead, he watched with irritation as she mounted her horse and rode away on the blue moonlit road.

My heart pounded like the tread of Portia's horse. It was finally just me and Quinten and he would never be more vulnerable. His army was asleep, his sorceress was gone, and he didn't even have a weapon. I straightened my stance and let the sound of my footsteps draw Quinten's attention.

"Who's there?" he asked, his body tightening ever so slightly.

I stepped in front of him, allowing the moon to light my face.

"Knox Duffy," I said.

Quinten's eyes squinted. He looked me up and down, then his face shed any worry it held.

"Yes, I recognize you. You're far from your village." Quinten rested his hands casually on his hips. "You need to return before danger befalls you."

He moved to walk past me and head back to his tent, but I stood firm, challenging him. "You're here for your father, I suppose."

"I'm here to kill you."

Quinten paused when he noticed the knife in my hand. He smiled, but I could tell his mind was still tumbling from his conversation with Portia.

"I have a whole army of men within shouting distance from here. Are you certain you want to do this?"

"I'm certain." My heart began picking up speed. Excitement coursed through me and I was surprised I wasn't afraid. "Any man can be as brave as you if he has an army to protect him and a woman that can injure men without even touching them. I want to see what you can do on your own." My face tilted toward him. "Plus, I know you're too proud to call for help."

Quinten cocked his head to one side and grinned at me curiously.

"If I recall, you should know how I fare on my own."

I twitched, remembering our encounter on the battlefield. I couldn't remember what happened after I blacked out and that made me less confident.

"It doesn't seem fair," Quinten continued.

"Have you ever fought a man one-on-one, equally matched?" I asked, taunting him, pushing him as far as I could.

He turned so that we faced each other straight on. He pulled back his shoulders and tilted up his chin. It was so easy. A proud man like Quinten would never be able to give up a chance to prove he's the best, even to a village boy like me.

"Are you aware that I killed the last Supreme Ruler? He had a horde of men to guard him!"

"I'm not sure you really did. Perhaps you had Portia do it for you. She seems far more deadly than you."

Quinten laughed, opening up his arms as if to say how ludicrous an idea that was. "Yes, well, you look half dead yourself so maybe someone as weak as me can take care of you." Quinten smiled. He wiped his hand along his bottom lip. "Perhaps this was your father's problem, not knowing when he's outnumbered."

He tried to be subtle, but I noticed his stance straighten. As I listened to him talk about my father, the wall that was covering my emotions tumbled. I charged him, raising my dagger as I ran. I reached for his throat but he blocked my arm.

"How did you do it?" I spat, our faces inches apart. "How did you become so wealthy, so fast?"

Quinten pushed me back by my shoulders. His temper flared.

"I know it wasn't honorable!" I swiped at Quinten again, aiming for his neck.

He laughed and I punched him, three blows, so he stumbled back. It felt good to fight again. It felt good to feel my skin hitting his. Quinten recovered quickly. He cocked his arm then pushed me back with one strong hit. I threw my right leg back to steady myself, but my knee buckled and I fell forward. Head bowed, Quinten kneed me in the face and I crumbled backward. My hands flopped to my side. The knife slipped from my grasp. I grappled for it, but my eyes were clouded with blood. Quinten stood above me. He stepped on my forearm so I couldn't reach my knife. His knee fell to my chest. Like an instrument of torture, his leg pinned me to the ground so that I could barely breath. I felt his smooth fingers on my cheek as he covered my mouth with his hand.

"Do you want to know how I became so rich and powerful?" Quinten whispered, his mouth close to my ear. "I know the man with all the rings." He said it in a sing-song way, enjoying every taunting word as it left his lips.

Quinten reached over to pick up my knife. With my free hand, I grabbed his ear and a patch of hair. I ripped my arm back as hard as I could. He tried to shift away from me, and as he did, his grip on my wrist freed. I kicked him off and rolled away. We both were back on our feet, but Quinten had my knife. He swung at me from up high. I ducked. He pulled away and swung again, this time aiming for my middle. I blocked him with my arm but he was stronger than me. I could barely hold the blade away.

With everything inside me, I lunged toward him, trying to push him and the knife away from me. My vision began to haze and I struggled to keep my focus. He was no longer fighting me. His mouth curled into a disgusted smiled. He considered me as I desperately came at him. I pushed and hit what felt like a stone fortress. My body was done. I was done.

"You're pathetic," Quinten said.

My body teetered on my feet and I reached out to steady myself on a nearby tree.

"Are you ready to give up?"

"No."

"C'mon, Knox!" he taunted. "I bet you're a lot like your father. He sacrificed himself for a good cause. Now you will too. In the end, this was the worst your father could do to me." Quinten pulled off his shirt. He revealed a myriad of half-healed slashes across his chest. Quinten wasn't quite as strong as I imagined him to be when we started fighting. His shoulders, arms, and stomach were covered in bruises and cuts.

My father, my father. I couldn't take hearing those words anymore. I rubbed my throbbing head. I wished desperately that I knew what happened in the space of time before I awoke in the woods. Quinten knew. He knew what happened with my father. If I killed him, I may never find out. I would never know how my father saved my life.

"Knox," Quinten said in mock endearment.

"What happened with my father?"

I stumbled toward him. My body knocked into him, a desperate attempt to harm him any way I could.

Quinten swung his arm. With the back of his hand he threw me to the ground. I landed flat on my back.

"Your father was an idiot."

"Please," I begged. "How did he die?"

"Die?"

I rolled onto my side, coughing blood onto the ground.

"How did you kill him?" I shouted, my patience ended. Quinten started laughing, a deep bellowing laughter that filled the trees. He looked down at me.

I was like a dying animal to him, a pathetic creature squirming in front of the hunter before it's killed, but I would die with dignity. I held Quinten's gaze as he said, "I didn't kill your father."

CHAPTER TWELVE

"COME WITH ME, village boy."

Quinten extended his hand to me. I hesitated, then took it as he pulled me off the ground. Grabbing the back of my neck, he led me through the woods. I was far too tired and delirious to fight back.

"Boy ..." I mumbled as we walked. "I'm not a boy."

"Just walk."

Quinten stopped, jerking my head and pushing me onto my knees. I bowed my head into the blackness. A quiet moan drifted to my ears. Quinten yanked my head to attention.

"This is why you're alive," he said.

Slowly, my eyes adjusted to the new shade of dark. I began to see the form of a man slumped and leaning against a tree.

"Father?" A shift in the leaves drew my eyes to the right. Another man sat a few feet away and next to him another.

I blinked away the blurriness of my fight with Quinten and saw that ten downcast figures lay before me. All were shackled at the wrists and ankles. Each man was linked together by an iron chain wrapped around the tree.

"Father!" I shouted.

Quinten let me scramble to my feet. He took a step away from me then watched with amusement.

"Father!" I said again for I wasn't sure if my eyes were tricking me. Was I delirious from the loss of blood? Was this a cruel joke Quinten was playing?

"Son."

I bent onto my knees, taking my father's face in my hands. It was him, the same square jaw and scruffy beard, but this figure was battered and bloody.

"You live," I breathed.

I felt his arms, though weak, reach up to hug me. The heaviness of his chains forced his arms back down.

"Who else is alive?" I asked as I stepped away from my father. Squinting my eyes, I searched for familiar faces.

"Sten? Hugh?"

"Sten survived," came a deep voice as Sten spoke for himself.

"What about Peter? Are you here?" I stumbled down the row of men. There were more than ten of them, fifteen, twenty, maybe more.

"I am here."

I found Peter and bent to look him in the face. His eyes were heavy. He was covered in dirt and blood.

"Neil?" I asked, hesitation in my voice. "Is Neil here?"

There was silence as the men struggled against their weaknesses.

"Neil did not survive," my father said finally. "At least he was not taken with us."

I turned to look at Quinten, who stood with his arms folded.

"Then I can guarantee you he's not alive."

"Your families, they think you're dead! Everyone thinks all of you are dead!" I said. I could feel my voice rising to a hysterical pitch.

It was as if I were the only person privy to a sick joke.

"Of course they do." Quinten's voice deflated my moment of energy. "I want their families to believe them to be dead. Soon you'll join these men, and your mother will eventually give up hope that you're ever coming home. Don't fret. While you're marching to the capital, at least you'll be with your father."

"But why? Why let them live?"

Leaves crunched on the forest floor as Quinten stepped toward me. One of his prisoners coughed.

"See, this is why I call you boy. You don't think like a man, like a ruler. I need only to give the illusion of dominance. That's why I kept our prisoners hidden. In case anyone, like you, came spying on us.

"These able-bodied men can still be useful to me. I need workers to build my new kingdom. Soon the castle that stands in LilyAye will be replaced with something better." Quinten took a step closer. "I told my soldiers, from the start of this trip, 'Kill the weak. Anyone who gives you trouble—they are the strong. Keep them for our work back home.'"

I looked down at my father.

"But your father ..." Quinten said as if he were reading my thoughts. "He was different. It's true, he was one of the strong. I was still set on ending his life since he almost killed me. So when I received help from my soldiers on the battlefield, I drew my sword on your father, but he began to beg."

I felt a chill run through my body. It was as if I were back in that moment.

"He begged and begged for the life of his son. Isn't that right, old man?" Quinten turned to look at my father, bending down as if he were speaking to a small child.

"Is that the truth, Father?"

"I did not wish for both of us to die." My father's words were quiet and choked. "I asked him to take my life if he would only spare yours."

"Why would you do that? I was in torture at the thought of your death!"

"Son." Silence laid in the air around me. "You have not yet lived your life."

"So," Quinten said, taking another step toward me, "I spared your life as your father asked. I let him bandage you up and hide you away from the rest of the battle. Instead of killing him, I kept him, and from now until he dies, he'll work for me, mining or building or whatever I want. Probably not the best decision I've made since now you've come back to cause me trouble."

Quinten flashed my knife, which he still had gripped in his hand.

"If you let me take you," he said, "you'll live, and you'll be with your father."

"I will not yield."

"Knox, no," said my father.

Quinten's face turned into an expression of irritation. "I'm getting tired of tumbling around this territory with you."

"I'm not done fighting," I said, standing up to meet his gaze.

The smile on Quinten's face dropped away. In a moment, he was on top of me, his hands around my neck. He stared intently as I gasped for air. I forced the muscles in my body to relax. Quinten did the same. In his moment of release, I screamed out and reached up to peel Quinten off. I punched him in the jaw knocking him on his back. He raised his hands to my throat, but I rolled over and pinned him to the ground. My fist swung at him over and over until Quinten brought his hands up to cover his face. My knife fell from his hand onto the forest floor. I grabbed for it, bringing it close to his neck.

"Don't," Quinten gurgled.

I drew my knife up to slice his throat. My heartbeat sped up. It felt as though someone was squeezing it between their fingers. Desperately, I clawed at my chest. "My heart."

Quinten threw me off. I crawled onto my hands and knees as Quinten kicked my knife out of my grip. I rested on my knees for a moment before collapsing to the ground. Quinten bent to pick up my knife and then stood over me, catching his breath. He spat blood from his mouth.

"Far too stubborn! Just like your father, but this time he can't save you."

Although I couldn't see them in the darkness, the trees above me rustled and swayed. My mind flickered back to when I woke up on the battlefield. The loneliness of that moment haunted me. I cocked my head to see Quinten. He met my eyes. His face contorted with rage, Quinten dove at me, extending his foot to kick me in the ribs. Then he came at me with the knife.

"Portia," I said, holding up a hand.

"What?" Quinten paused.

"Portia. Please, stop. I know something about her."

"You don't know her! No one knows that woman."

"Please." I looked over at my father while still holding onto my chest. "Let me live and I'll help you control her. I know she can't die," I added.

"How do you know that?"

"Because I killed her." I took a deep breath. "I killed her the day of the battle. Yet she still lives."

Quinten looked away from me and sighed. This was the secret he didn't want anyone to know. I realized then that this might give Quinten more of a reason to kill me. Then his shoulders slumped and he seemed calmer. I moved into a seated position and wiped blood away from my nose.

"I don't need to control her."

"Yes, you do." My breathing was labored. "She's stronger than you and you want to know where she goes when she runs off."

Quinten's eyebrows furrowed.

"I can help you. We grew up in the same territory. I know where her family lives. I know who her husband is. I know who her children are."

"She truly has children?" Quinten asked.

I nodded.

"What are their names?"

"Knox. Don't," my father said.

My eyes flitted to the mass of shackled bodies.

"Tuor is the boy. Then she has Camilla, a little girl."

Quinten crossed his arms. I slowly pulled myself up to my feet, watching to see if Quinten would allow it.

"I can follow her," I said. "You have a country to run, so you can't watch her. I know you want to know where she is and what she's doing."

"I can send one of my soldiers to do that."

I shook my head.

"No. You can't, because you don't want your soldiers knowing who she is."

"Do not bargain with this man!" My father's shout came strained but desperate.

Quinten stared intently as if he were challenging me on what I had just said. I had already figured it out and his reaction confirmed what I already knew. Portia was the reason that Quinten was Supreme Ruler. Maybe she used her powers to kill Bradac. Maybe she used some sorcery to help him build an army. I wasn't quite sure how, but I knew Portia was at the core of it.

My breaths were heavy as I waited for him to reply. He could still kill me.

"Why should I use you?" He rubbed the spot on his jaw where I had hit him.

I rested my hands on my knees, letting air fill my lungs. My mind debated against itself. Quinten didn't know how Portia really felt about her children. For all he knew, she loved her children and visited them when she could.

"Her children," I said.

"Knox, no! Leave the children out of this!"

I swallowed hard, my eyes locked on my father's pathetic visage. Quinten's nerves seemed frayed. In a blink, he barreled toward my father, taking his hair in his hand to stretch open my father's neck.

"I think it's time you shut your mouth and let your son speak!" Quinten took the tip of my knife and placed it in the curve right under my father's jaw line. "Continue," he said, turning back to me.

"It's not worth it, son," my father said. "You'd rather die than use the ones you love."

"Shut up!" Quinten shouted. He pushed the blade closer to my father's skin so that a stream of blood formed on his neck.

"Okay!" I said. "Stop!" My voice was shaky. "Her children, she never speaks of them?"

"Not often," Quinten said, his teeth tight together.

"It's because she cares for them. She fears for their well-being. She knows that being wrapped up with you is a danger to them."

Quinten's eyes burrowed into me. It was a lie. I knew from Belle that Portia didn't care at all for her children. I just had to convince Quinten that she did if this was going to work. My father's eyes closed; he knew there was nothing more he could do to stop me.

"I know the woman who looks after her children. Tuor and Camilla are Portia's weak spot and I have access to them, with no suspicion."

I waited, staring expectantly. Quinten's grip on my father loosened. His eyes were alight with ideas. He could now capture, torture, or kill Portia's children if he thought it would get Portia's attention. I looked down at my hands. They were quivering and covered in blood. I imagined the blood wasn't my own, but that of Tuor and Camilla. Guilt infiltrated every part of my body. I didn't want Quinten to harm these children. In that moment I secretly vowed that if I made it home alive, I wouldn't let Quinten touch them.

Quinten let go of my father, patting his head in a

mocking way before standing. "Very well," he said. "Return to your village and tend to your wounds. I will send a rider soon with your instructions. Let me make this clear," Quinten wiped the blood from my knife on the leg of his pants. "When I tell you to make a move, make it." He handed me my knife, blade first. "One false step, and I will kill your father."

CHAPTER THIRTEEN

I LEFT CAMP that night with only the things I had arrived with. It took me half of the next day to stumble back to my village. I didn't go to my parents' house. I didn't go to my home in the swamps. The first place I went was Belle's. I was so delirious when I stumbled through her front door, I could barely speak. Somehow she got me upstairs to one of her bedrooms and cleaned and bound my wounds.

When I woke the next morning, I was happier than I'd been in almost a year. Belle entered the room as sunlight caught on her sandy blonde hair. She had an apron secured around her waist as usual. She wasn't wearing any jewelry and her face wasn't painted, but she was the most radiant woman I'd ever known.

"I just got back from seeing your mother and Rebekah," she said, bending down to pick something up off the floor and stuffing it in the pocket of her apron. "They were both sick with worry." Belle untied her apron and laid it across the bed frame before sitting on the bed to face me. "Rebekah went down to your house yesterday and then came here to look for you."

"Belle."

"Your sister said she barely slept last night."

"Belle, please."

"What happened to you?" Belle's face was scrunched with deep worry.

"My father is alive."

Belle sucked in air and covered her mouth with her hand.

"Peter Lindon is alive, too, and Sten, and Hugh Kloeter. Quinten took them as prisoners."

"But how? How do you know that?"

"I followed Quinten and his army."

"What about Neil?" she asked, dropping her hand. I shook my head.

"Neil wasn't there, but some of our men live and we can bring them home."

"How did you get away?"

I shifted awkwardly underneath Belle's knitted blanket.

"I barely fought my way out."

Belle's eyes fell to my knife, which she had carefully placed on the table next to my bed.

"Will you go and tell my mother he's alive?"

"Of course." Belle bowed her head to stare at her fidgeting hands. "Knox ..." Her gaze turned back to the table. Next to my knife was Belle's book that I always kept in my pocket.

She picked it up, pulling out the fragile dried flower that lived between its pages. "Why do you have this?"

I felt a lump of guilt catch in my throat. "This is the flower I wore in my hair the day Neil and I married." She paused. "Am I right?"

"Yes," I said finally.

"Why do you have it? I cried when I lost this."

"That day I came over after your wedding, I asked if I could borrow a book. I watched you press that flower between a stack of books so it would dry. So you could keep it. I saw you do that and I just stole it."

"But why?" she asked, almost hysterical now.

"Because it was torture! It was torture watching you two together. I just couldn't handle it. I thought I would take the flower and destroy it, but then I couldn't. Why do things have to change?"

"Simply being alive means seeing things change." She set the book back on the table.

"I wanted us to work things out. I just can't let Bear Gap continue on like nothing happened," I said, pushing myself up to a sitting position. "Many men still died and I'm determined to avenge their death and to keep this territory the way it's always been."

Belle sighed, shaking her head slightly.

"You need to let this go. You and I can't change what's happening to our territory. We can't stop Quinten's initiative."

"I don't agree with that." The words came out scratchy and drawn.

"Knox ..." She looked at me with intense eyes. "You're not really angry with Quinten Warwick." She paused, letting those words seep into my mind.

I pushed the thought away at first and then I remembered where my anger had gotten me.

"You're angry at yourself."

Belle was smart, always intuitive. I wanted to be mad at her for saying that, but how could I argue with the truth? She was right. She always knew me better than anyone. I thought that if I killed Quinten it would justify what had happened to my father and my family.

"I know," I said, unable to debate against Belle's warm blue eyes.

"We don't agree on how to deal with Quinten." Her eyes left her lap and found their focus on my face. "But you know I care for you a great deal."

I took a shaky breath and said the thing to Belle that I should have said a long time ago. "I'm sorry."

Belle reached up to touch my cheek.

"I'm just so sorry," I said. My head was wrapped in bandages, along with my arm and my knee. It hurt to move. I wrapped Belle's hand in mine.

"I'm sorry," I said one more time. My throat tightened.

"You know I've always loved you. I always will," Belle said.

Belle's eyes glistened too and I felt my body calm at the sound of her speaking. The skin on her hand was smooth compared to mine. I linked my fingers through hers and let our hands fall to the bed. Belle leaned in, bringing her other hand to the back of my neck. Gently but without hesitation, she placed her lips on mine.

I touched my hand to my chest, the area where I had become so used to feeling the quickening beat of my heart. Instead of feeling an unnatural rhythm, I felt a peace, and the steady calm of my faintly beating heart.

EPILOGUE

THE AIR IS warm and muggy. It's summer. I run the blade of my sword along the whetstone. When I'm finished I'll clean the blade and return it to its spot on the mantel. Then I'll pull out another sword and continue the ritual. My arsenal is strictly decorative. None of my weapons have been used for anything outside of giving me something to do, something to fill my time.

It's been seven years since the Battle of Bear Gap, since my father was captured. After my fight with Quinten, it only took him a few weeks to catch up with me so I could fulfill my promise. He sent a messenger to Bear Gap to find me and give me my first assignment. The messenger held a sealed letter from Quinten giving me specific instructions on how I was to follow Portia, carefully tracking her every move, and then I was to report everything I knew back to him.

Once production started on Quinten's big farm, he had houses built in town so the flood of new workers would have a place to live. I was one of the first to be assigned one of these homes, since I was a servant to the Warwick government. From this house I watched my territory morph. It has become crowded, not just with villagers but with Warwick soldiers too.

The farm: Quinten's great institution that he is now famous for. It took several years to implement, but once he brought on a governor in Bear Gap, someone likeminded to himself, he was able to feed the nation. Quinten swiftly relieved all the territories of their seed, keeping them completely reliant on our farm. Now, when the weather is bad or Quinten's ships have damage, many people go hungry because the food can't reach them in time. To Quinten, it's brilliant. He's created a nation completely dependent on him. Many people love him and the ones who don't are fully reliant on him, so it doesn't matter if they like him or not. I have become the very thing I hated, a cog in Quinten's wheel.

For years I tracked Portia. Sometimes I was gone for six or nine months at a time before I could get any information on her. Then in a blink, she would be untraceable again. Sometimes she would live contentedly in the castle in LilyAye with Quinten, allowing me to come home and work at the farm to make some rings. The Supreme Ruler doesn't bother with me much anymore. Occasionally, I'll get called up for a mission, but Quinten's rule has become strong.

I look down at the mark on my arm and scratch at it absentmindedly. It's a big sprawling brand that is a replica of the Warwick crest. Our new governor started demanding all workers receive a brand as a way to keep us accountable. If you don't have a brand, then you can't get onto the farm to work. If you don't work, you don't get paid, and since there are now so few other ways to make money in our territory, the brand means survival.

I find myself thinking about Tuor and Camilla often. Occasionally, I see them working at the farm. Camilla's so young, barely a teenager, but there are children younger than her working the fields. Belle still takes care of Tuor and Camilla whenever she can. Even Belle, with the inherited wealth of her father, now struggles with the shift in the economy.

Things with Belle have never fully ended. She isn't married, and neither am I. We have never talked of marrying each other. Being away on my missions for Quinten made it difficult to make Belle happy. Shortly after the battle, she gave birth to Neil's child, a girl. Belle keeps quite busy with her daughter. She told me once that she would always love me, even if we were estranged. I did eventually tell her about my arrangement with Quinten. When it became too hard to keep it from her, I told Belle how I'd used Tuor and Camilla as a means to save my life. That conversation was a catalyst in our relationship. She was furious and told me she could never trust me again. I don't fault her for losing confidence in me. I was never quite worthy of Belle anyway.

From time to time, I'll see Camilla pass by my house. I swear I see her being followed, being watched. I'm certain Tuor is too. Quinten keeps his spies on them. They're incredibly subtle, blending into this town as farm foremen or shop owners. I have realized that I was only the beginning of Quinten's secret task force against Portia. The more powerful she becomes, the more paranoid Quinten becomes. He keeps an eye on her children, her husband, anywhere she's been, or anything she's touched. I think Quinten is just waiting. Waiting for the moment he is going to strike.

I, too, wait for my moment to strike. Seven years later and my father is still a prisoner in LilyAye. I know he's alive because it's the only thing Quinten can use to keep me working for him. My promises have started to sound like vain musings. I tell my family over and over that I will bring John Duffy back to Bear Gap but most days I just feel ... paralyzed.

These days I'm happiest on my little front porch, in my little Warwick-owned house. I have a rocking chair and a book in hand, one of the many that I borrowed from Belle's troves of books. When I feel my heart picking up pace, spinning out of control, I force myself to be calm. I think of my porch and my rocking chair, and if I have to, I think of Belle.

THE END

Pronunciation Guide

CHARACTERS
Camilla: Kuh-mil-uh
Tuor: Toor (like tour)
Bradac: Bra-dak

PLACES
Elmyra: Ehl-meye-ruh
LilyAye: Lilee-eye

Want to know what happens next?

Knox's story does not end here. Visit www.emilyfortney.com to explore the entire Camilla Crim series and grab your **FREE** eBook by signing up for Emily's email newsletter.

***

If you enjoyed this book, please leave a 5-star review on Goodreads or the online retailer where you purchased it. Also, pass this book on to a friend. Good books are meant to be shared.

EMILY FORTNEY is the author of the Camilla Crim series. Currently living in Pennsylvania with her husband, Emily is passionate about dark chocolate, Earl Grey tea, and her cat.

Emily absolutely LOVES hearing from her readers! Connect with her over at www.emilyfortney.com